Nasty Breaks

Charlotte and Aaron
ELKINS

Nasty Breaks

THE MYSTERIOUS PRESS

Published by Warner Books

A Time Warner Company

Mysterious Press books are published by Warner Books, Inc.,
1271 Avenue of the Americas, New York, NY 10020.

Visit our Web site at http://warnerbooks.com

A Time Warner Company
The Mysterious Press name and logo are registered trademarks of Warner Books, Inc.
Printed in the United States of America
First printing: November 1997

10   9   8   7   6   5   4   3   2   1

Library of Congress Cataloging-in-Publication Data

Elkins, Aaron J.
     Nasty breaks / Aaron Elkins and Charlotte Elkins.
         p.   cm.
     ISBN 0-89296-596-7
     I. Elkins, Charlotte. II. Title.
   PS3555.L48N3   1997
813'.54—dc21   97-23487
                                                                                CIP

Acknowledgments

Sad to say, the Quonochaugachaug Public Golf course and the Mooncussers Inn are fictional. Other establishments and locations on Block Island are real, and we thank John and Leslie Sisto of the Book Nook in Old Harbor for showing us the lay of this lovely chunk of rockbound New England coast.

Chief William McComb and Sergeant Troy Reynolds of the New Shoreham Police Department set us straight on island police matters and patiently answered our slew of generally queer questions.

And Joe Gores, fellow mystery writer and marine-salvage expert, generously filled in some of the many gaps in our knowledge of deep-sea diving.

Nasty Breaks

Prologue

Up through the dark waters he rose, trailing bubbles, like some black, buoyant monster from the depths. Seen from the deck of the *Virginia II,* he was like a great marine flower growing and foaming and blossoming before them as he neared the gray, rain-pocked surface of the sea.

His face was turned up, the two men under the awning on the deck could see that through the water, turned up and joyful, and even before he broke through he had torn off his face mask and mouthpiece, so that he was laughing and choking and trying to talk all at once as he groped for the ladder on the side of the boat. The two men above looked down at him and laughed too, although they weren't sure what they were laughing at yet. Whatever it was, Andy had come up with good news, and they were more than ready to laugh about that.

Once he had hooked one arm over a rung, he held up a squat, thick, greenish drinking glass in his other hand. "Stu, Benny—Look!"

The two men on the boat whooped. Benny Trotter, at forty-five the oldest of the three, leaned over the side, snatched the tumbler out of Andy Gottlieb's hand, held it to his own unshaven, grizzled face for a sloppy kiss, and brandished it over his head like a man who'd just gotten his first Oscar. And when Andy clambered over the side, clumsy in his wet suit and huge flippers, the three of them embraced and did a crazy little jig around the cluttered deck while the rain came down on them.

They had plenty of reason to celebrate. The last time a human hand had touched that glass, Thomas Jefferson had been in the White House. Since then, for nearly two centuries, it had lain undiscovered on the seabed below, a mere one hundred yards off Block Island's isolated Black Rock Point. The glass had been manufactured in the year 1807 in Boston. On March 2, 1808, it had been loaded aboard the bark *Good Hope* in Newport under the supervision of Captain Elijah Todd for its two-year voyage to the other side of the world. In addition to ninety-four crates and thirty barrels of glassware, the hold of the *Good Hope* had been richly stocked with shovels, spades, flour, tobacco, beer, and cutlery, all bound for Canton.

But on its first evening out of Newport, driven off course by a sudden, violent nor'easter, the *Good Hope* had broken up and gone down in the ancient ship's graveyard off Block Island's rocky southwest coast, where the emptying waters of Block Island Sound collided with the endlessly seething North Atlantic.

All this the three men already knew. They had pored through the *Good Hope*'s bill of lading in the marine museum at Mystic, Connecticut. They had read newspaper accounts of the disaster in the *Boston Gazette*. And now, after two years of on-again, off-again attempts to locate it, they had finally found the wreck itself. It was, they knew, potentially the richest find of their four-year association, the Big One, the one that would finally let them buy a decent new boat and some up-to-date equipment: sonar, an underwater magnetometer, a reliable underwater camera, maybe even a submersible—or, as long as they were dreaming, make that a video-equipped submersible. Who *knew* what this might be worth?

But there had been other "Big Ones" before, only none of them had panned out. Through the years they had managed more or less to cover their costs and earn enough besides to stay ahead of their debtors, but little more. The *Good Hope* was their ticket out of the minor leagues of treasure-hunting dilettantes; it would put them on the map as serious, reputable salvage divers.

If a substantial amount of the Colonial glassware and cutlery was still whole and recoverable.

That was what Andy had been down there trying to determine. They had spotted the wreck four days before—or not the wreck itself, but a fifty-foot-long, roughly rectangular area of scattered stones and jumbled cannon that they excitedly recognized as ballast from a nineteenth-century ship. Near it was a long, ill-defined mound on the seafloor, eight feet high in places. In a single day's work, taking turns below, they broke into the mound to discover the ship itself, or what was left of it, lying on its side, entombed in a thick concretion of mud, sand, and petrified sea life. Since then, working from dawn to dark each day, they had been engaged in the hard, dangerous task of trying to find their way to the cargo hold through an unstable mass of collapsed and collapsing timbers buried under tons of mud. And now Andy had done it. Peering by the light of his lamp between two rotting timbers, he had glimpsed a seabed strewn with neat clumps of glassware, as if the crates had rotted around them and the glasses had simply settled gently to the ocean floor, right where they were, and never moved in the hundred and ninety years since. He had picked up the first undamaged piece he'd found, this sturdy, humble drinking glass, as whole and perfect as if it had come from the factory the day before, and hurried up to show them.

"They're just *sitting* there," he told the others, still trying to catch his breath. "It's fantastic, wait'll you see!" He tinkered with his face mask and straddled the gunwale, preparatory to letting himself back into the sea. "I'm going back down; we need to shore up some stuff."

Benny Trotter, still clutching the glass to his chest, beamed happily at the leaden sky, lost in fuzzy dreams of wealth and fame. "Doo-dee-doo-dee-doo-dee-doo," he crooned softly.

"Bad idea," Stuart Chappell said to Andy. The thirty-two-year-old Stuart, youngest of the three, was in many ways the most mature. Andy tended to be a little impulsive and devil-may-care. Benny could be unfocused and rambling, and had a way of seeing the world through rose-colored glasses. But Stuart was serious, analytical, and persuasive, and it was he who had emerged as the natural leader, insofar as there was any leader at all. "It's been a long day, Andy, let's not push it. Tomorrow's another day, buddy. We'll rig up the sling, and we'll work hard, and we'll all get rich."

"Yeah, sure," Andy said, "but—"

"And anyway, the weather's getting downright nasty," Stuart said.

"That's true," Benny said, reluctantly coming back to reality. "The storm's really brewing up now."

As if to make his point for him, the boat juddered as a five-foot wave slapped against the hull, sending a surge of water onto the deck. There were whitecaps and flecks of foam all around now, and the *Virginia II* had begun to toss and wallow. They were perilously close to the offshore rocks, some of which were visible, but most of which lay unseen a foot or so beneath the surface, and they knew that if the storm really got going and the anchors didn't hold, which was a distinct possibility, the *Virginia II*, a twenty-seven-foot, thirdhand, converted lobster trawler, could be flung against those jagged rocks in seconds and dashed to pieces. Stuart and Benny exchanged a glance that said it all: if it could happen to the *Good Hope*, it sure as hell could happen to them. On the rocky beach, in fact, lay the shattered, inverted body of another vessel, a fishing trawler that had been caught on the rocks a few years before, its splintered frame naked to the darkening skies.

But Andy was hardly one to look on the dark side. "Hell, I'm afraid it's going to cave in down there if we let it go till tomorrow. It could take us days to dig it out again. And what would happen to those glasses? Look, if I can't get it done in an hour, I'll come up. Okay?"

Stuart started to speak, hesitated, and sighed. "You'll come up the second we tug on your lifeline?"

"Absotively." Andy grinned, pulled his mask down, and adjusted it. "Pozzolutely." Into his mouth went the mouthpiece to the "hookah," the air hose connected to the on-deck compressor. He climbed a few steps down the ladder, waggled his fingers in a cheery goodbye, and dropped with a velvety splash into the darkening water.

"Ah, hell," Benny said, doing his best to work up a reassuring smile, "don't worry about Andy, Andy knows what he's doing." He was still holding the glass, absentmindedly now, rotating it in his fingers. "He's only thirty-five feet down, Stu. Everything'll be just fine."

*   *   *

Everything wasn't fine. Twenty minutes after Andy went

down, the storm closed in with a vengeance. Icy gusts of rain whipped the awning aside and pelted the men. The boat rose and fell, sometimes with a foot-jarring *splat*, on steep salty swells. Long, mottled combers boomed against the nearby rocks, erupting into twenty-foot explosions of water and foam.

In another five minutes there was a new motion in the deck beneath them, a halting, grinding vibration that made both of them freeze and stand stock-still, their heads alertly tilted, listening, waiting. The tremor came again. The *Virginia II's* anchors were dragging. They were being sucked toward the rocks.

"Get him up," Stuart said shortly, starting for the wheelhouse. "I'll get us cranked up."

Benny nodded tightly. He pulled on Andy's lifeline, went pale, and pulled again. "Stu!" he shouted over the storm and the steady *putt-putt-putt* of the compressor. "Stu! My God!"

Stuart hurried back. "What's wrong?"

For answer, Benny tugged on the lifeline. "It won't move!"

Stuart grabbed it out of his hands and pulled hard. "It's caught on something." He pulled again, with both hands, arching his body backward. Nothing happened. He tried pulling on the air hose too, more gently because if it, too, was hung up on something, pulling too hard on it might kink it and cut off Andy's air supply.

He shook his head. "No good. They're both caught." The boat jerked again, eight or ten feet this time, toward the rocks.

Benny stared at him and licked his lips. "What do we do?"

"We have to get out of here," Stuart said.

"But . . . but . . ."

It wasn't necessary to explain the *buts*. If they pulled up the anchors and headed away from the rocks toward open water, they were almost guaranteeing Andy's death. He was down there inside the tunnel, not on the open ocean floor. The air hose would snap, or kink, or be pulled from his mouth; the lifeline would crush him against the walls of his cave under the sea and trap him there, or drag him, airless and tumbling, over the sea bottom, or wedge itself deeper into whatever chink it was already caught in and perhaps collapse the tunnel onto him.

Stuart, suddenly raging, cut him off. "What are we supposed to do?" he screamed with the rain soaking his eyebrows and pouring off his face in runnels. "Is it going to save him if we let ourselves get dragged into the rocks? *Is it?*"

The boat dragged again. Another ten feet toward the rocks. The pounding waves thudded in their ears. Benny looked sick to his stomach. "Stu . . ."

"We have to cut him loose," Stuart said. "That way he'll have a chance. If he makes it to the surface we'll see him."

"Cut him loose?" Benny echoed.

But Stuart was finished talking. With quick, concise movements he pulled the end of the lifeline free, then used his diving knife to cut the air hose.

Benny watched, unprotesting and defeated, chewing on the knuckles of one hand. At the whoosh of air from the severed end of the hose he jerked. "God help us," he whispered.

Stuart scowled at him and ran for the wheelhouse.

* * *

Andy twisted onto his back and aimed his light upward and to the right, trying to see through the straggling weeds into the hollow that was worrying him. It didn't look good. All that seemed to be holding up the "roof" on this part of the tunnel was a five-foot-long, square-cut beam about ten inches on a side—a section of the keelson, probably—that was thick enough to do the job but that was spongy to the touch and riddled with teredo burrows besides. Damn, he thought, they were going to have to waste half a day—

A split second before he felt the convulsion in his lungs the steady, reassuring rumble of his exhaust bubbles suddenly ceased. Before he was able to make sense of this, a mallet seemed to smash him in the chest, driving out most of the air he had left. He stopped up his breath and closed his windpipe at once, hauling vigorously on the lifeline to get himself out of there. But the line was snagged in the vertex of two fallen timbers a few feet behind him. Panicky and suffocating, he tugged desperately at it, his body writhing. He never knew that it was his own foot that kicked the section of keelson out from behind him and brought forty tons of mud and timber down on him, crushing out the last few cubic centimeters of air in his lungs.

And if he had known, what difference would it have made?

Chapter 1

The Present

Lee Ofsted leaned both hands on the kitchen counter and addressed her dinner. "Beef tortellini parmigiano," she told it reproachfully, "is not supposed to be gray."

It wasn't her fault, she knew that. She had followed the recipe to the letter. ("Remove plastic lid from Serv-a-Bowl®. With fork, perforate foil cover. Microwave on HIGH for four minutes. Remove foil and **ENJOY!**") And still the stuff was an unappealing gray. Not grayish or gray-brown, but gray, and a mushy, fibrous gray at that, about as appetizing as wet particleboard.

The picture on the label ("Serving Suggestion") didn't look anything like wet particleboard. The chunks of beef were a tawny brown, the pasta a creamy gold, the cheese a delectable ivory with just a hint of toastiness at the edges. The label looked delicious. So much for truth in advertising, she thought grumpily. The label probably tasted better too.

She crunched a stalk of celery and considered walking to Seventeenth Avenue for a decent sit-down dinner at El Palenque, but that would mean getting into street clothes and eating by herself in a restaurant, neither of which she was in the mood for. It would also mean an unscheduled, unallocated dent in her budget, and she was even less in the mood for that.

These gloomy and unproductive thoughts were interrupted by a chirp from the telephone on the rickety stand in the living room. All things considered, a welcome diversion. Lee picked it up on the second ring.

"Hello?"

"Lee? I'm glad I got you. This is Peg!"

The identification was unnecessary. Peg Fiske's friendly, cheerful foghorn of a voice was not the kind you were likely to forget. Lee smiled and held the receiver away from her ear. "Peg, aren't you supposed to be at golf school? In Connecticut or someplace like that?"

"Rhode Island. Block Island, actually, which is this wonderful island they have off the coast. Look, are you doing anything important right now?"

"Not really. I was cooking my dinner. Or rather, looking at it. Or rather, talking to it, if you really want to know the truth."

"What?"

"Nothing. What's up, Peg?"

"Well, first of all, you *are* between tournaments at the moment, aren't you?"

That was one way to put it. Lee, starting her third year as a pro in the Women's Professional Golf League—the WPGL—generally tried to play in every tournament she could get into, as did most of the other young, struggling, not-yet-prime-time players. If you didn't play you couldn't earn anything. But this week's competition was the Myrtle Beach Invitational. And the Myrtle Beach Invitational was what it said it was—an invitational event, not an open one, which meant that there was no Monday qualifying round or any other means through which the younger, less-established pros could compete for entry slots. The Myrtle Beach was restricted to the top forty money-winners of the previous year, period. And that failed to include Lee Ofsted. Unfortunately it wouldn't have helped her any if it had been the top fifty either. Or the top seventy-five. Now, if they'd been more broad-minded and had just opened it to the top one hundred and fifty . . .

"Yes," she said, "I'm between tournaments."

"Great. You're not going to believe this. First of all, forget dinner—"

"I wish I could."

"What?"

"Nothing. What am I not going to believe?"

"Stop mumbling, will you? For heaven's sake. Now, pay attention. Here's what's happened. The program doesn't even start officially until tomorrow, but one of the instructors already slipped a disk getting a bag down from the luggage rack on his plane and won't be able to teach, so they need a replacement. And so naturally I told them all about you, and they positively leaped—"

"You want me to teach at a golf school? You're out of your mind. They wouldn't want me, believe me."

"But they do, they do. The minute I mentioned your name, Jackie—he's the head instructor—said he thought he might have heard of you."

"Wow," Lee said, laughing, "am I as famous as all that? Look, I appreciate this, Peg, honestly. I know you're trying to do me a favor, but it wouldn't work. A teaching pro and a touring pro are two different animals. Being good at one doesn't necessarily mean being good at the other. In fact—"

"Yes, yes, yes, yes, yes," Peg said impatiently, "I know all that, you told me a hundred times, but this is different."

"I'm telling you, I'd be lousy. I have a natural swing, remember? *I* don't really know how I do it, not when you get right down to it, so how could I teach it to somebody else?"

"I understand, but—"

"And besides that, the last thing I want to do is pick my swing apart to see how it works and maybe mess it up and my whole career along with it—lackluster as it is at the moment."

"Lee, will you listen, for gosh sakes? That's the beauty of it. You wouldn't have to do swing basics. Jackie does that himself. You'd be teaching the short game—chipping and pitching and putting. You've told me yourself the short game's different; nobody's a natural at it. There are exercises and techniques you can pass along. Am I right?"

"Well . . ."

"Of course I am. I ought to know. You've given me enough help with it. What do you say?"

"I say thanks, but no thanks. Teaching just isn't my—"

"Graham's in Paris, isn't he?"

"Don't remind me."

"And you don't have to leave for your next tournament till after the weekend, do you?"

"No, but—"

"And the job here's a snap. You'd just teach an hour or two a day, then go around the course with them, giving them some coaching, and that's it. And you'd be done early because it's just this funky little nine-holer. Five hours a day, tops."

"And do what the rest of the time?"

"Nothing. Whatever you want. The practice range here is pretty good, and you can spend all morning on it if you want, balls supplied. And listen, they'll fly you out and back business-class, they'll cover all expenses for the week, and they'll pay you a thousand a day besides. What more can you ask?"

Lee blinked. "A thousand *dollars?*"

"No, a thousand zucchinis. Of course, a thousand dollars. That's five thousand all together, which is a lot of airplane tickets for the rest of the tour, as I don't have to point out."

She certainly didn't. Five thousand dollars was about what a twentieth-place finish in a typical tournament would earn her; less than she dreamed of for herself before the start of the first day of play, but better than she usually wound up with on the last day. Five thousand dollars would more than cover her expenses—food, motel, travel, entrance fees, caddie wages—for the next three tournaments, so that any winnings at all would put her not only into the black but well into the black, not a condition that she enjoyed very often.

"Well . . ."

Peg, sensing Lee's crumbling resolve, pressed on. "Not only that, but Stuart Chappell, the man who's footing the bill for everything, is sparing no expense. We've got this great old inn, all to ourselves—Block Island is real Old New England, you'll see—and the chef is fabulous. We haven't even officially started yet, so tonight he just 'threw a little something together' for the early arrivals. Well, it was veal scallops in wine sauce—absolutely fantastic—and tomorrow for the official kickoff dinner it's going to be filet mignon in béarnaise sauce."

Lee flicked a quick glance into her kitchen, where the Serv-a-Bowl® was sinisterly biding its time on the counter. Whatever béarnaise sauce was, it was sure to be a big step up from beef tortellini parmigiano.

"You know," she said, "it might be fun at that."

"Atta girl!" Peg, never one to hide her emotions, was transparently pleased. So was Lee, when it came down to it. The two of them were good friends despite their coming from such sharply different worlds, and it wasn't often that they could spend a few days together.

"Now, then, there's a United flight that leaves Portland tonight at eight-thirty-eight your time," Peg told her. "Can you make it all right?"

"I can make it."

"Good, your ticket'll be waiting. You transfer at Chicago and arrive in Providence at six-thirty tomorrow morning. I'll be there to meet you; we have a fleet of rental cars here at the inn for us. It's about a two-hour drive, including the ferry ride, so there'll be time for a bite and a good gossip on the way to the island, and you'll have a chance to clean up and have a nap before the program gets going."

"Fine."

"Good, I'll tell you more tomorrow. Sorry about your having to take the red-eye."

"No problem," Lee said brightly. "Bye, Peg, see you in the morning. And Peg . . . thanks."

The first thing she did was toss her congealed dinner into the garbage bag under the sink. The second thing was to call Domino's and order a salad and a deluxe pizza with everything on it, even anchovies, to eat while she was packing.

At a thousand dollars a day, she wasn't about to deny herself a little princely living.

Chapter 2

Indeed, the red-eye flight was no problem. Golfers in Lee's budget category were used to traveling at all hours to get from one tournament to the next. More often than not, a carful of them would drive all night to reduce costs, taking turns at the wheel. In the jargon of the trade they were known as "rabbits": golfers who were good enough to qualify as pros on the WPGL tour (and thus certifiably among the best two or three hundred women golfers in the world), but not good enough to do anything but nibble at what was left after the bona fide superstars— the Laura Davieses and Dottie Mochries and Betsy Kings—drove and chipped and putted their way to the rich, green rewards of top-notch golf.

Not *yet* good enough, anyway. And until they were, those who didn't have rich parents or generous sponsors lived a carpetbagger's existence on the fringes of the golf world: breakfasts at donut shops; dinners at places with signs that said "Eat"; lodging, sometimes three or four to a room, at Motel 6 or Super 8 or whatever local motel was willing to give the golfers a break. And long, long nights of barreling down dark highways telling themselves that *this* was going to be their week at last.

Given all that, hurtling quietly across the country at 39,000 feet in a wide, soft, business-class seat was a snap. And it was a pleasure, for a change, not to be fretting about some tournament she was on her way to. All she had to do for the next five days was give a few short-game lessons, do a little friendly coaching—and collect her $5,000. And there would be ample time to put in some unhurried, unpressured time on the range, smoothing out the hitch that had cropped up again at the top of her swing.

A paid vacation, that's what it was going to be.

By the time the plane crossed the Rockies, Lee was sleeping like a baby, her feet tucked up under her.

✻ ✻ ✻

It had been four months since she'd seen Peg, but their catch-up session lasted only the time it took for a coffee stop in Wickford Village, a Colonial town (not a Portland-area shopping mall with fake Colonial buildings, but a real, living village with an eighteenth-century church, narrow streets, and pretty row houses with little plaques that said 1709 or 1735 or 1799) twenty minutes south of the airport. The thing was, the two women moved in such utterly separate spheres that there just wasn't much to catch up on. It was amazing that they were friends at all, really. They had met at a pro-am tournament a couple of years earlier, and for whatever strange reason, they had simply clicked. Sturdy, chubby, reliable Peg Fiske, Lee was somewhat surprised to think now, was probably her best friend.

On second thought, forget the "probably." Who else was there?

But their lives could hardly have been more different. Peg was going on forty-four, Lee was going on twenty-four; Peg lived in a posh golf course community near Santa Fe, Lee lived in a cluttered, tiny apartment above Aunt Mollie's Things 'n' Stuff in Portland's old Sellwood District (although actually she seemed to spend most of her life in motels); Peg ran her own $500,000-a-year management consulting business out of Albuquerque, Lee—well, Lee wasn't doing quite as well as that. The only person in Peg's world that Lee considered a friend was Peg, and the only person in Lee's world that Peg considered a friend was Lee.

As a result, there was hardly anyone or anything to gossip about. Peg had been happily married to her physicist-husband for fourteen years, after all, so there was hardly likely to be anything new on that score. As for Lee's love life, it had been pretty scarce lately, to put it mildly. Her one and only ex-Carmel-detective-lieutenant-turned-security-consultant Graham Sheldon, was in Paris, of all places, conducting a training program for a group of car-manufacturing executives on how to deflect terrorist kidnapping attempts. Before that it had been Milan. Before that, Mexico City. Before that—

"It's really something," Peg mused, stirring a second spoonful of sugar into her coffee, "how that business of his has taken off. He's been at it how long, six months?"

"Seven." Lee slowly shook her head, remembering. Out of the blue he had handed her a business card:

Countermeasure, Inc.
Consultants in Personal and Corporate Security
Graham T. Sheldon, President

He was quitting the police force and going into business for himself, he had told her with a happy smile. It had knocked her for a loop, but it had pleased her too.

"It seemed like such a good idea at the time," she told Peg, "but the problem is he's so good at what he does, and he's so damn presentable . . ."

"That's a problem? I should have such problems."

"No," Lee said with something between a laugh and a sigh, "I mean the whole point was that as a consultant he'd be able to make his own schedule, he'd be able to join me on the tour whenever he felt like it—but instead he's had one client after another. If anything, we see each other *less* than we did before."

"Well, if you ask me," Peg said, "it's better that way. Would you really want Graham to be tagging along after you like some kind of a—a groupie instead of having a real career of his own?"

"No," Lee said. *Yes,* she thought.

"And besides that, you have your own career to worry about. You need to concentrate on golf, you know that. In the long run, this'll work out better for both of you, mark my words."

"As long as he doesn't find all that jet-setting around *too* attractive and forget all about me," Lee grumbled.

"Lee," Peg said soberly, "let me tell you something. Never, not once, have I seen Graham Sheldon even glance at any woman but you. If ever a man was in love, it's him. And the man's adorable. Count your blessings, my girl."

"You're prejudiced," Lee said, but she smiled gratefully. There was no one else who could cheer her up and make her see things straight the way Peg could.

"Well, naturally I am. Who wouldn't be? The guy's a gem." Peg put her cup into its saucer with a clatter. "We'd better get moving if we're going to catch the seven-forty ferry."

"So tell me about this golf school," Lee said as they climbed back into the car.

Peg complied happily and at length. The program was being

put on for the management staff of SRS—Sea Recovery Systems—a Boston-based firm that had carved out a niche of its own as a broker of marine salvage services: when a tanker ran aground or broke apart somewhere in the world (which happened a great deal more than one would think, according to Peg), or when deep-sea emergency towing was needed, or when an offshore oil rig unexpectedly required maintenance, the firm that needed help would contact SRS, which would then use its worldwide, up-to-the-minute, computerized tracking system to locate the closest available salvage ship or marine equipment that could do the job, then radio the necessary instructions to it. Within minutes, assistance would be on the way. And SRS would have earned itself a commission.

The idea had been the brainchild of a man named Stuart Chappell, back in the 1970s. He was a dissatisfied young marine engineer at the time, Peg understood; he had chucked his career to go into salvage diving—treasure-hunting, really—and after the usual failures he and his partner had finally hit pay dirt, so to speak, off the Block Island coast with the wreck of the *Good Hope*, an early-nineteenth-century cargo ship loaded with glassware and cutlery. Stuart's partner, already middle-aged, had sold his share to Stuart and used the money to open an inn on Block Island, almost within sight of the find. Stuart had used his eventual profits to start SRS, or rather the one-room, punch-card-machine operation that was eventually to become SRS. The idea had found a ready clientele, and although imitators had soon come along to challenge it, SRS's recently installed communications technology had reestablished it as the acknowledged leader in the field, with affiliate offices in Tokyo, Sydney, and London.

Not being a man to forget old ties, Stuart had been holding his company's annual executive planning retreat at the inn of his old partner and friend—the Mooncussers Inn, on the outskirts of Block Island's Old Harbor—for a decade or more now. This year there were seven people in attendance, including Peg.

"Their executive retreat is a golf package?" Lee asked. "Talk about job benefits."

"Not usually, no, but this year, yes. It's a combined golf-instruction package and organizational-restructuring meeting."

Lee laughed. "Now, there's a nifty combination."

"Well, that's Stuart for you," Peg said, smiling. "He's a one-of-a-kind. And he has some . . . well, depending on your point of view, you could call them either fairly progressive or fairly nutty ideas when it comes to executive development. The golf bit is supposed to develop positive thinking and problem-solving."

"Uh-huh, and it also just happens to provide a tax-deductible, five-day vacation, right?"

"Now, don't be cynical, it doesn't suit you. I think he's really serious. Well, serious for him. He loves going to executive seminars, you see—Cornell, Harvard, NYU—and every time he comes back from one, he's all worked up about some new cure-all that's going to solve all their problems. Sometimes they're a little extreme. They tell me that last year he had his people go through a desert-survival course that was supposed to teach them mutual trust and interdependence."

"Did it work?"

"The only definite results I heard about were two cases of heat rash and one sprained ankle when someone jumped ten feet in the air and came down on a rock after sitting on a Gila monster. And then, when he decided to try the idea of executive staff meetings every Friday to clear the air, Stuart hired this Zen guru to sit in on them and instruct them in the ways of peaceful co-existence—"

Lee laughed. "You're kidding."

"—but the guy got into a shoving match with one of the department heads, and now there's no more guru and no more weekly staff meetings either."

"Brother."

"But don't get the wrong idea. Stuart's not dumb, he's smart. He built SRS from the ground up. It's just that he's suddenly discovered team-building and human relations and all that sort of thing, and it's sort of overwhelmed him, if you know what I mean."

"Not exactly, no."

"Mm. Well, it's an occupational hazard, from what I can tell. I've known it to happen to engineers before, especially after they've been managers for a while. At some point, after years of metal-stress calculations and thermodynamics, they suddenly come to the amazing conclusion that people are important too; that to run an organization you have to give all kinds of thought to motivation, psychology—"

"Which you do, don't you?"

"Yes, of course you do, but unlike the rest of us who knew it all along, these people go overboard, and the result is desert-survival courses and gurus. But he's a good egg, Stuart is, even if he is just a little, ah . . ." She paused, her head cocked.

"Unorthodox?" Lee suggested. "Unconventional? Eccentric?"

Peg shook her head to all of them. " 'Cracked' is what I was looking for. Fortunately his wife, Darlene, otherwise known as the Grand Czarina, is one tough cookie, as hard-nosed as they come, and she doesn't let him stray too far off the deep end." She glanced over at Lee. "A word of advice, by the way: you do not, repeat not, want to get on Darlene's wrong side."

"You mean she'll be there? She's attending?"

"You better believe it. They couldn't get along without her— in her opinion, that is."

"And how come *you're* included in this thing, Peg? Is the company a client of yours?"

"As of two months ago, yes. I did an executive reorganization and compensation study for them and made some tentative recommendations, which Stuart has had the good sense to follow to the letter. And Stuart, being Stuart, thought that a good way to introduce the changes would be during their annual retreat, where they could begin working out the new relationships in a totally stress-free environment. Which, incidentally, strikes even *me* as a pretty good idea, not that there's any such thing as a totally stress-free environment. And I understand that making the golf-instruction part of the package was Darlene's idea. Don't ask me why—but it certainly shows that the woman can't be all bad."

"Will you have a lot of work to do, Peg? Meetings and things?"

Peg nodded. "That's the price I have to pay, but I'm not complaining. After all, I get to attend the golf instruction too. Stuart asked me if I wanted to, and I told him to go ahead and count me in."

"Naturally," said Lee with a smile. Peg was probably the most avid golfer she knew, or at least the most avid consumer of golf instruction in all forms: courses, videotapes, books, gadgets. If she had ever passed one up, Lee didn't know about it. Not that it seemed to help much, but it kept Peg happy, it helped keep the merchandisers solvent, and compared to a lot of other things it was pretty harmless.

While Peg talked on, Lee, still a little sleepy—it wasn't yet 5 A.M. Oregon time—lazily watched the scenery slide by. Only the morning fog reminded her of home. Compared to Oregon, the Rhode Island landscape was small-scale, almost miniature: shrimpy trees, no mountains—not even anything a westerner would think of as a self-respecting hill—but pretty to look at all the same, a gentle, rolling, New England countryside, full of meadows and woods, with tidy villages and handsome, old, shingled houses behind stone-and-iron gates, and ancient, low stone walls winding everywhere, even through the woods. And always, shimmering through the bright, thin fog, the luminous, blue swath of Narragansett Bay.

It was all very restful, very soothing. Lee had been to Rhode Island only once before, to play in a two-day, non-WPGL tournament at the Winnapaug Country Club course near Weekapaug, or was it the Weekapaug Country Club course near Winnapaug, or . . . ?

"Anyway," Peg was rattling on, "I have to be at a supercritical meeting at nine, which I should just about make by the skin of my teeth if I'm lucky, and I told Jackie you'd meet him in the dining room about a quarter past, so that he can give you a little orientation before the golf program starts at ten." She glanced at her watch. "That'll just give you time to shower and change into golf clothes. No nap, I'm afraid. Is that all right?"

"Sure, it's fine. I slept on the plane," Lee said, yawning. "What's your big meeting about?"

"Oh, it's an organizational thing. You wouldn't be interested."

"Sure, I would. Of course I would. Don't you think I'm interested in your work?"

"Okay, then. Until now, all of SRS's top managers have been equals, reporting directly to Stuart. This is not good. It makes for one messy situation after another, with crossed lines of authority, muddy communication channels, dual or even triple responsibility, and various other unpleasantness. The reason they hired me was to fix all that, you see?"

"Mm-hm," murmured Lee.

"Well, one of my recommendations was the creation of a new position of executive vice-president, to which all of Stuart's other top managers would report. So at the meeting this morning Stuart will announce which one of them he's picking to be the new executive veep—who, by the way, will receive a very substantial increase in salary and perks. Now, since all four of them are hoping to get the job, and what's more, feel that they *deserve* the job, there's going to be some frustration and some hard feelings, and I want to lay the groundwork for working out the interpersonal and intraorganizational stresses and for fostering an atmosphere of teamwork and cooperation that . . ."

She peered suspiciously at Lee. "Hey, are you awake? Lee? Lee . . . ?"

* * *

They caught the ferry at a briny little dockside town with just one street to speak of, consisting almost entirely of commercial lobster-fishing wharves more or less alternating with seafood restaurants that smelled fabulous even at this time of the morning. "This is Galilee," Peg told her as they waited to board the ferry for the seventy-minute trip to Block Island.

"Galilee? What's the name of the town across the inlet over there, Bethlehem?"

"Close." Peg laughed. "It's Jerusalem, as a matter of fact." She held up her hand, traffic-cop style. "Don't talk to me for a minute now, I have to concentrate. This guy is actually motioning me to *back* onto the boat. He's taking his life in his hands."

The *Anna C* wasn't Lee's idea of a ferry, but then the only ferries she was really familiar with were the stately, green-and-white giants of the Evergreen Fleet that glided back and forth across Puget Sound in her neighboring state of Washington.

Broad, slow-moving vessels, wide-open at each end (so that they didn't have to turn around and drivers didn't have to back on or off, which saved a lot of stress), the Evergreens had space for over two hundred cars on the auto deck. And on the upper decks, besides all the comfortably padded, nicely decorated seating areas, there were two heated solariums, a big, full-scale restaurant and (naturally, this being Seattle) a Starbucks espresso bar.

All things considered, the Washington ferries had more in common with the *Queen Elizabeth 2* than they did with the *Anna C*, an unpretentious little ship with room for two dozen cars and a few hundred foot passengers, and with dining amenities pretty much limited to a snack bar. But it was a real ship, very nautical—the front end came to a point—and there was something about its plain, old-fashioned, strike-the-main-gaff-topsail atmosphere that suggested that it was prepared for heavier waters than Puget Sound.

It didn't take long for Lee to see why. Block Island Sound was a sound in name only. As far as she was concerned, these were the open seas, and once they'd gotten beyond the breakwater that enclosed the Harbor of Refuge, the ship began to heave slowly, regularly, up and down. Lee wasn't a terrible sailor, but she wasn't a great one either, and the motion soon began to get to her.

"Uck," she said.

Peg looked up from her *Providence Journal-Bulletin* and cherry Danish. "Mm?"

"I think I'm getting a little queasy."

"Really? Why don't you try reading something to take your mind off it? Make believe you're on a train."

"Good idea." Lee opened the tourist pamphlet she'd gotten from one of the racks.

Block Island, named for the Dutch explorer Adriaen Block, who first set foot on it in 1614, has been the setting of dramatic shipwrecks for more than three centuries. Its rocky shores and swelling, rolling, storm-tossed seas . . .

She closed the pamphlet. "I don't think so."

Peg glanced at her. "Oh dear, you do look a little green around the gills. Maybe you should lie down for a while?"

Lee nodded and lay back on the bench, as several other gray-faced passengers were also doing. She crossed her hands on her abdomen and closed her eyes.

"We'll be there in just a little while," Peg said sympathetically, through a mouthful of cherry Danish. "Less than an hour."

It didn't sound like such a little while to Lee. "Whoo," she said, and concentrated on making her mind a blank.

* * *

The moment they reached the protected waters behind the long arm of Block Island's Lantern Rock breakwater the ship stopped heaving, and Lee perked up and opened her eyes. "Did I make it? Are we there?"

"Welcome back to the land of the living," Peg said, smiling. "Pretty, isn't it?"

Lee sat up as they approached the dock. It was pretty, all right. The fog had thinned out and the Victorian cupolas, turrets, and gingerbread-trimmed mansard roofs of Old Harbor gleamed dainty and bright against a crisp, blue sky with a few scudding clouds in it. From the edge of the quaint little town a broad, sandy, impossibly immaculate beach with a few strollers on it stretched in a shallow arc to the foot of low, sand-colored cliffs a couple of miles away. The whole thing was almost too perfect to be real, a life-sized, color-enhanced picture postcard.

"It's lovely," Lee said, and then after a moment, "Thank you, Peg." *Thank you for pulling strings to get me hired, and for calling me up and convincing me to come, and for getting me out of my dumpy little apartment and my feeling-sorry-for-myself little sulk,* she meant.

Peg laughed. "Better not thank me until you see the golf course."

When they were back in the car, waiting for the signal to drive off the ferry, Lee asked: "By the way, what's my boss's last name? Jackie what?"

"Didn't I tell you? Jackie Piper."

"Jackie Piper." Lee's jaw dropped. "Not the character that does those television what-do-you-call-'em, infomercials? The guy with a gadget to cure every golfing ill known to man?"

"And to woman too," Peg said. "I should know, I've got a garage full of them. Practically his whole Stroke-Cutter line."

"And have they ever cured anything?"

"Now, don't be like that, Lee. Jackie really has a lot of good ideas. This school is going to be just what I need," Peg told her earnestly. "My game's going to improve a lot as a result of this."

Lee couldn't help laughing. It was a never-ending source of amazement to her that a hardheaded, down-to-earth, eminently sensible businesswoman like Peg could be so . . . so judgment-impaired when it came to golf; Peg and a lot of other people, all of whom truly seemed to believe that there was some untried device out there, if only they could find it—some contraption that kept your hips from turning in advance of your shoulders (or vice versa), or a golf club that made rude warning noises at you if swung on an outside-to-inside plane—that would turn them from 40-handicappers to graceful, smooth-swinging scratch players.

"Well, I hope so," Lee said agreeably. "I'll certainly do my best to help. Tell me, is Jackie Piper as, um, lively in person as he is on TV?"

Peg grinned. "More so. He's a real cutie-pie. I swear, you just want to chuck the little guy under the chin and carry him home with you." At a signal from a crew member she turned the key in the ignition. "Ah, here we go. Just pray he doesn't expect me to back *off*."

Once off the boat, Peg turned left on Water Street, driving past the Harborside Inn with its sunny front terrace full of breakfasters, past the Inn at Old Harbor, past the Star Department Store ("Gifts, Souvenirs, Salt-Water Taffy") and the Seaside Market, all comfortably housed in spruced-up 1880s-era buildings. It was still early in the morning, and not yet into the full tourist season, but there were enough browsers and shoppers from the mainland to make the place lively and inviting.

At the first intersection, by the hundred-year-old statue of Rebecca at the Well—once a drinking fountain with basins on different levels for people, horses, and dogs, but with its seven tubs now filled with potted plants—they swung onto Spring Street, winding their way uphill past bigger and grander old hotels—the Manisses, the 1661 Inn, the Spring House Inn. Once beyond the top of the rise, the inns got smaller and less grand, relying more on homey charm than imposingness. The Mooncussers Inn was one of these, an old, two-story clapboard house, lovingly tended, with dormer windows on the upper floor and a roomy wraparound porch complete with flower boxes, rocking chairs, and even a porch swing.

But if the outside was turn-of-the-century farmhouse, the inside was turn-of-the-century motor launch. The lobby was minuscule, no more than twelve feet by fourteen, but it was outfitted like Captain Nemo's drawing room, with charts on the wood-paneled walls, a collection of navigational instruments of lovingly burnished brass and steel, and not one but two antique world globes on floor stands. Behind the inlaid teak desk was a grandfatherly, comfortably overweight man with a pink scalp showing through thinning white hair, a well-barbered white goatee, a nose like the bulb of a turkey baster, and merry blue eyes that put Lee instantly at ease.

"Hiya, Benny," Peg said. "Here she is, your latest guest. Lee, this is our host, Benny Trotter, proprietor of the Mooncussers, master of the premises, and distinguished country gentleman."

The man got up laughing. "All that, and I also unstuff the toilets when they get plugged up, let's not forget the little things." He put out a plump hand to Lee. "Pleasure, Miss Ofsted. Hope you enjoy your stay." He spoke with a lovely tenor voice, creamy and melodic, almost as if he were singing.

"I'm sure I will." She gestured at the surroundings. "This is wonderful. It's like a museum."

Obviously, it was the right thing to say. Benny lit up. "Well, that's just what it is, don't you see? Just look around you. Do you see a single reproduction? A 'genuine copy'? An 'authentic facsimile'? No, ma'am, you do not. Everything, even this paneling on the walls"—he rapped the dark, burnished wood with his knuckles—"came off of real, seagoing ships—ships that went down, as a matter of fact. Right in these waters, as a matter of fact. Now, you take this little object here." Into her hand he plumped an eight-inch-long, square-sided copper spike that had been serving as a paperweight on his neat desk. "What would you say that is?"

Lee hefted it; it was surprisingly heavy. "US" was stamped into the metal on one side. "Um . . . one of those things you hammer into railroad ties?"

Benny laughed. "Now, that's not a half-bad guess, but it's not right. That's my Paul Revere spike, is what that is."

"Your Paul Revere spike?"

"Hey, you two," Peg cut in, "I'm sorry to break this up, but maybe we'd better let Lee get up to her room. She's been riding on a plane all night and she has to be all bright-eyed and bushy-tailed in about fifteen minutes. I know where her room is; I'll show her up."

Benny laughed again and put the spike back on his desk. "Well, if you figure out how to get bright-eyed and bushy-tailed in fifteen minutes I sure wish you'd let me in on the secret." From the ornate but much-damaged open cabinet behind his desk—a Chinese whatnot, he called it, from a Boston trader that broke up off Cat Rock Cove—he pulled a key that was attached, like the other keys, to a weathered piece of wood or ivory with a crudely etched sailing ship on it. His lively blue eyes watched her, waiting for her to comment.

"Is this scrimshaw?" she asked tentatively.

"Scrimshawed whalebone," he said proudly. "From the *Mary Elizabeth*, out of London, lost with all hands between here and Cape Cod in 1831."

Lost with all hands. Lee looked at the gray, weathered object in her hand. Who spent his spare hours carving it during a long voyage? Someone's husband? Someone's father? Were his bones still on the sea bottom between here and Cape Cod? "I hope you'll have a chance to tell me more about some of these other things later," she said sincerely.

Benny positively glowed. "Oh, well," he said as he sat back down at his desk, "I'll see if I can't make the time."

"Well, you sure made a friend there," Peg said at the top of the stairs. "Look, I have to run, they're waiting for me. Remember, hon . . . Jackie downstairs in the dining room at nine-fifteen, and then you need to be out on the range by ten, which is when the golf instruction starts, unless somebody happens to murder somebody else at my session."

She clunked hurriedly downstairs. "In which case," she called back up as an afterthought, "it might not be until ten-thirty."

*   *   *

The guest rooms at the Mooncussers Inn had names, not numbers, and according to the brass plate on the door, Lee's was the Bowsprit Room, but there was nothing nautical about it other than the name. The walls were covered with muted, green, floral-patterned wallpaper, the furniture old and well used, the bedstead made of gleaming, elaborately curling brass. There was a rocking chair, an old mahogany bureau with a tilting mirror, a small, round table and two little, well-padded Victorian chairs in the sunny, angled nook created by one of the dormer windows. Everything was old, but everything was spotless. The only thing up-to-date was the white-and-salmon-tiled bathroom.

On the doorjamb was proof that the place had had a previous existence as a family homestead, and that the Bowsprit had once been a young boy's room. There was a column of straight, horizontal lines scratched into the honey-colored wood, with words and numbers next to them: *Roddy, June 1929; Roddy, January 1930; Roddy, June 1930* . . . climbing all the way up to 1938, where the highest scratch mark was about five and a half feet off the floor. The fortunate Roddy, whoever he was, had grown from a child to a young man in this sunlit room.

All in all, it was a wonderful place; she already felt at home here, not that home had ever been remotely like this. Peg had told her that the rooms went for $250 a night, and no wonder. She stepped into the alcove created by the other dormer window and looked out over the open countryside to the southeast.

Lord, it was beautiful, stark and beautiful at the same time, like pictures she'd seen of Ireland, a sweeping landscape of farms and grassland rolling to the shore, and glinting ponds and lovely, isolated, old farmhouses, and those endless low stone walls everywhere, winding down into valleys and up over hills, and always the closeness of the sea. It was enough to raise the spirits and soothe the mind at the same time, a whole lot better than sitting around her apartment in Sellwood moping about her finances, her love life, and her career. Plus three tournaments' worth of funding to boot, let's not forget about that.

Life was good.

Chapter 3

Inside the two-hundred-year-old cottage the hulking man sat with his hands in his pockets and the windbreaker zipped up to his massive neck. He hated the cold. The windows had been open all day to the warm May breezes, but the old house had stood unused and unheated since the previous summer, and it was going to take a while to get rid of the dank chill that had seeped into walls and floorboards during the long, fierce, New England winter. He had tried fooling with the stubborn knob on the old steam radiator against the wall but had failed to get any heat out of it.

More successfully, he had used the 1950s electric percolator to make a pot of coffee from the opened can of Maxwell House that had been in the refrigerator since God knew when—the fifties was as good a guess as any—and had even located a cup of crusted-over sugar in a kitchen cupboard and a Tupperware container with a dozen petrified shortbread cookies, no longer chewable in the usual manner but capable of being more or less mashed between the back teeth after sufficient dunking.

For almost an hour now he had been sitting, chilled but otherwise reasonably content, at the scarred table in the sparsely furnished main room, sipping, dunking, and mashing, absorbed in an old *Reader's Digest* condensed novel about the haughty, beautiful daughter of the Duke of Burgundy and how she was abducted on the high seas by a dashing pirate (in actuality a wrongfully dispossessed nobleman of the neighboring Duchy of Luxembourg) who didn't know her real identity but thought she was the servant of a humorously cranky middle-aged woman (who was actually *her* servant).

The chirp of the telephone, wouldn't you know it, came at just the wrong moment. The disguised duke's daughter was just about to confront the dispossessed nobleman with a golden ring she had found in his cabin (which she was sharing with her maid at his insistence), the crest on said ring proving beyond any doubt the fact of his noble birthright.

Still, business was business and the fact of the matter was that he surely hadn't come to this godforsaken piece of rock in the middle of the ocean to catch up on his reading. He put the book down and picked up the phone.

"Felix's Snatch Service," he said brightly. "Results you can rely on."

The receiver practically jumped out of his hand. "Dammit, Felix, don't *do* that! What are you, you out of your mind? Are you crazy? I could have been anybody!"

"Well, excuse me for living," the fat man said, stung, but then decided it was only good sense to keep relations cordial. "I'm sorry, I was only trying to be funny. But after all, how could you be anybody but you? That's who you are, if you know what I mean."

"How could I . . . ? What is that, a joke? Is that what this whole thing is to you, a joke?"

Felix rolled his eyes toward the water-stained, acoustic-tile ceiling. The people he had to deal with. No sense of humor, not a shred. The voice at the other end continued blatting unpleasantly away: "And what took you so long to answer? Where the hell were you? Is something wrong?"

"Nothing's wrong," he said reassuringly. "What could be wrong?" The man was practically a nutcase. "So what do you say?" he asked. "Are we on for today or aren't we?"

"We're on, of course we're on. Is everything set? Do you have the truck gassed? Do you know where to be? Did you—"

"*Please,* I know my trade. You just do your part—you make sure she's there—and everything will be fine."

"I will, she'll be there, all right. But I don't want you to take any unnecessary chances, understand? Everything has to be absolutely perfect. There's too much riding—"

"What kind of chances?" Felix interrupted hotly. "Will you please, for God's sake, relax?"

Not that Felix wasn't a little nervous too; it was only natural under the circumstances. But was there any need to go to pieces? "If things don't work out on the second hole," he said, "then we hold off until the fourth and make the snatch then. If not the fourth, then the eighth, right?"

"Yes . . . Felix . . . seriously . . . I wish you wouldn't refer to it as . . . I mean, I wish you'd stop calling it . . ."

"A snatch? Well, really, what would you call it?"

Honestly, the man was going to make *him* crazy before this was done. The thing is, if he had known he was going to be dealing with this crackpot he'd never have taken on the job in the first place. His original contact person was fine, real businesslike, but *this* character was about six apples short of a picnic. And what was he so scared about? It made Felix nervous that he'd never seen him face-to-face. He'd seen his partner, the other one, but not this guy. Why not? What, the guy didn't trust him?

"How about not calling it anything?" he was saying now. "How about . . . ah, look, it's just that I . . . oh, hell, I've never done anything like this before."

No! Good heavens, what an absolutely, mind-boggling surprise. "Which is why you're paying me," Felix explained, seeing if logic might help. "So you might as well let me do the worrying."

"Yes, but are you sure *you* know what you're doing? Have you ever pulled off anything like this before? Tell me the truth for once."

Felix chuckled. "Be serious, will you? A hundred times, maybe more."

Well, once, not that it was quite the same as this job, and not that it worked out exactly as planned, for that matter, but how was Felix supposed to have known that the bag with the ransom money had only a thin layer of real bills on top, or that it had one of those bird-dog tracking gizmos in it and was bugged besides, or that the "courier" that brought it was actually a detective, or that two video cameras were recording everything that went on? That little mix-up had cost him three months in the clink, which might have been three years if he hadn't had all that information to share with the D.A. He'd still be inside, if not for that.

But that was then. This was now, and he was older and wiser.

"Trust me," he said, "she's as good as sn—"

"Felix!"

". . . in that truck right now. There won't be any problems, believe me."

Well, there wouldn't, would there? Everything was arranged, every single angle had been taken into consideration. Every aspect had been worked out ahead of time, and the whole thing wasn't that complicated to begin with, was it?

What could happen?

Chapter 4

Lee wasn't sure that she was quite willing to give Jackie Piper absolute-cutie-pie status, but she could see what Peg had meant. He was one of those small, quick, agile men who don't seem to age like larger, slower people. That is, he looked his years—fifty or so—but with a perky, boyish, bright-eyed sparkle that made him seem like a fifteen-year-old doctored up with a few fake wrinkles and a little unconvincing gray in his hair to play some old geezer in the high school play. A lively, darting sort of boy-man, with fresh-faced, bursting-at-the-seams vigor to spare.

"Well, hel-*lo!*" he chirped, bouncing nimbly into the homey, deserted dining room and flinging himself into a chair at her table. "You just *have* to be Lee Ofsted! Am I right?" He offered her an ear-to-ear grin, with his eyes as well as his mouth, genuinely cordial from the look of it.

"Yes" was all she got out before being swept away by the avalanche of words.

"Thank you so much for coming! I can't tell you how grateful I am to you for helping us out. I just don't know what I would have done if Peg hadn't recommended you. Now, first of all I want you to know that I've checked your stats in the WPGL handbook, and I'm *very* impressed. I have complete and utter faith in you. I expect you to teach your part of the program in your own way, there's absolutely no need to adopt my approach, although you're very welcome to, and you can feel free to make use of any of my Stroke-Cutter aids at any time." He took a quick breath.

"Thank—"

"Now, here's our daily schedule: ten to eleven, swing basics and imaging techniques, which I'll be handling, but it'd be nice if you were there today at least, is that all right with you? Eleven to twelve-thirty, short-game instruction from you—chipping today, if you please, pitching tomorrow, putting on Wednesday, general coaching, review, and problem lies on Thursday and Friday. Twelve-thirty to one-thirty, lunch. In the afternoon, there's nine holes of golf for all who want it—probably a threesome and a foursome, or maybe two threesomes—during which you go around with one of the groups, freely bestowing Ofsted's Helpful Hints as needed. Then you're on your own until the social hour, where I'd just like you to be friendly and act your charming self—they always appreciate that kind of thing. Social hour's at six, dinner's at seven. There now, how does that sound to you?"

She listened, or tried to listen, with growing wonder. Could human beings really talk this fast? She'd seen his infomercials, of course, and had assumed without really thinking about it that his presentations were somehow mechanically speeded up. She'd also assumed that the astonishing pace was prompted by the need to make his every minute count. But here he was, live and in the flesh, with no commercial clock running, and he was twittering away in a state of high-octane energy overdrive that left her dumbfounded, miles behind him.

"Well," she said as her mind more or less caught up, "it sounds fine, I guess."

"Absolutely. Piece of cake." He spread his arms. "Sweetheart!" he cried.

It took her a surprised moment to realize that he was calling the waitress, a beefy, thick-legged woman of forty who was cleaning up the remains of the participants' breakfasts. "Sweetheart, honey, would you come over here, please? We're in a terrible hurry, and I haven't had any breakfast, and my blood sugar is at an all-time low, so do you think we could get some coffee and one of those wonderful sticky buns? You'd like one too, wouldn't you, Lee? A treat definitely not to be missed."

"Well, I already—"

"Make that two, darling, thank you so much. Chop-chop, now, move that cute little fanny!"

Coming from someone else, this probably would have earned him a punch in the chops, but delivered as it was in Jackie's puppy-friendly manner, all it got from the waitress was a girlish laugh before she left to get the order.

"You're going to have a wonderful time, Lee, it's an absolute ball! And these are really a fun group of people . . ." And off he went again, burbling away nonstop.

He *was* kind of cute, Lee decided. Not that she had any desire to chuck him under the chin, let alone take him home—more than half an hour of him at one time would be pushing it—but she did find herself, to her considerable surprise, liking him.

From what she'd known of him before, she hadn't expected to. He had been on the pro tour himself for a while, and although he'd done all right, he hadn't made it big enough to suit himself and had eventually dropped out of sight. Then, about five years ago, he had resurfaced with an instruction book called

Imaging Your Way to Better Golf. In it, he had simply collected many of the old mental-imagery golfing nostrums—imagine that you're swinging while standing in a barrel, imagine that you're swinging a bucket on a rope, imagine that your right elbow is strapped to your side on the downswing—added a few of his own, and put them in a three-hundred-page coffee-table book, one to a page, each beautifully illustrated by a top-notch golf illustrator.

The book had probably done no better than a hundred other similar manuals, but Jackie then took it one logical step further: if golf addicts were willing to pay $29.95 for *pictures* of "imaging," then what would they pay for the real thing? Why imagine you were standing in a barrel when you could stand in a real barrel (plastic) that actually gave you on-the-spot feedback when you swayed or dipped against its sides? Why imagine a bucket on a rope when you could practice with a real bucket (filled with a sealed quart of sand) on a real rope? And so the Jackie Piper Stroke-Cutter line of practice aids ("Not available in any store!") was born and Jackie found his niche as a television pitchman. Branching out to running high-end golf schools had been a natural extension.

Over gulped coffee and buns, Jackie gave her a loose-leaf program guide, quickly filled her in on the details, and asked her if she had any questions but didn't wait for an answer. "It's almost ten," he announced. "Time to face the music."

He jumped up, grabbed Lee's hand, and pulled her to her feet too. "Come along, you can ride with me to Quonochaugachaug."

"To *where*?" Or had he sneezed?

He looked at her. "The golf course? What you're here for? Hello? God help us, she's forgotten already."

"Quonochaugachaug is the name of one of the golf courses?"

"The *only* golf course. Where do you think you are, Myrtle Beach? It's nine holes and we're lucky to have that many. Believe me, God did not create the geology of Block Island with golf in mind."

He tugged impatiently at her hand. "Come-come-come-come-come, it's a five-minute drive." He jumped up, grabbed Lee's hand, and enthusiastically pulled her out of her chair. "Chop-chop!"

Obviously he could hardly wait to get started himself, but as they got to the door he stopped short and smacked himself on the forehead. "Holy mackerel, would you believe I almost forgot the most important thing?"

The most important thing, it turned out, was to inform her that the entire line of Stroke-Cutter training devices was on sale to the attendees at 15 percent off list price, and anything she herself sold to one of them would earn her a 20 percent commission.

He beamed at her as if he'd bestowed the rarest of privileges, and she fumbled for something to say. "Um, on list price or discount price?" was all she could come up with.

"Discount price, you little devil, what else?" he said, throwing back his head and laughing uproariously. "Please, lady, I'm trying to make a living here."

✿   ✿   ✿

The Quonochaugachaug Public Golf Course, which had been reserved for SRS this final week of the off-season, before the Memorial Day weekend and the Invasion of the Summer People converted Block Island from a sleepy, backwater community of eight hundred peaceful souls into a summer-long madhouse with ten thousand visitors a day, was what Jackie had implied, an eccentric little affair tucked into the nooks and crannies of the natural landscape wherever it would fit. Most of the fairways were nothing more than unmanicured swaths of heath and meadow, hummocky, boulder-strewn, and open to the whistling gusts that swept over the ten-square mile island from the Atlantic to the Sound. The whole thing was gorgeous, inspiring, and just about unplayable. The very first hole had its tee box atop the bluffs that paralleled the shore, while the fairway lay eighty feet below, on the winding, constricted shelf at their base, so that the rough on one side was just a narrow, stony beach; on the other it was sheer, eighty-foot cliffs. And the green, if you could call it that, was compacted sand, not grass at all. A heck of a hole, fun to play if you were in the right mood, but did it really have anything to do with golf?

She smiled, remembering an exchange she'd heard about between Bob Hope and Arnold Palmer after they had played a round together. "What did you think of my game?" Hope asked. "Pretty interesting," Palmer was said to have replied, "but personally I prefer golf." That was a pretty good summary of how she felt about Quonochaugachaug.

She had seen similar courses before, and although she admired the ingenuity and determination involved in carving them out, she had no burning desire to play on them, let alone try to teach anybody anything on them. But the course's practice facility, where she would be doing her teaching, was more than adequate, with chipping and putting greens (real grass), a bunker area, and a roomy three-hundred-yard driving range with grass tee boxes lined up almost at the cliff's edge, with glorious ocean views in three directions. Beside the first of these tee boxes, in a warm, fragrant breeze off the Atlantic, eight white plastic chairs had been pulled into a semicircle in preparation for the start of instruction.

"How'd you get along with Jackie?" Peg asked as people were taking their seats.

"Fine, how'd your meeting go? You look a little frazzled."

"My eyebrows are a little singed, that's all, but I think everything's settled down." She gestured with her chin in the direction of one of the managers, a spindly, pinch-faced man who seemed to have his hands full deciding on the best place to sit. "Malcolm Labrecque, the newly crowned executive vice-president of Sea Recovery Systems."

"*That's* the new veep?"

Peg smiled. "Malcolm believes in weighing all available options before committing himself."

"I'll say. How did the others take the news?"

"About the way you'd expect. Lots of warm, heartfelt congratulations for Malcolm, only the smiles were just a little rigid . . . like about two degrees this side of rigor mortis, you know? I think they all honestly expected to get the job—and now they're all nursing bruised egos."

"Wow, you do have your work cut out for you, don't you?"

Peg lowered her voice to a bare whisper. "To tell you the truth, I'm not at all sure Stuart made the right choice. Malcolm's great with macro-organization design, and techno-organizational subsystems, and all that—he knows more about them than I do—but he's hopeless when it comes to people. A zero, no interpersonal skills whatever." She shook her head. "I'm surprised Stuart picked him. I just hope it works out. In the meantime, I'm hoping Jackie will get them all thinking about other things for a while."

That he did. Within a few minutes, doing nothing more than going through the administrative details—teaching hours, refreshments, meals, course privileges—Jackie Piper had the people in seven of the chairs laughing, more or less relaxed, and in the palm of his hand.

The eighth was Lee, laughing along with the rest, but beginning to get a little queasy too. Who was she kidding? How in the world could she follow an act like this? After Jackie's slick, professional patter, she was going to look like a complete nincompoop. She was no performer, no teacher. Even as a little girl she'd hated getting up to speak in front of a group, and she hadn't changed all that much since. What had made her think she had the gumption to pull it off, let alone the ability?

Well, fair was fair; she knew the answer to that. Five thousand dollars.

"This is all your fault," she muttered ungenerously to Peg, who sat beside her.

Fortunately Peg didn't hear. She was listening to Jackie, who was now handing out white, stick-on labels with "Jackie Piper Golf Schools" prominently displayed in block letters.

"You want to put your names on these and wear them at all times," he was saying. "It not only helps me keep everybody's name straight, it's a safety measure that our insurance company appreciates. You're going to be hitting several hundred golf balls a day, and during past programs some attendees have wandered off in a fatigued state. With these on, honest local rustics will find you, identify you from your badge, and hopefully return you to us."

Without even pausing for them to laugh, he went on, as surefooted as a veteran stand-up comedian, which in a way he was. "And finally, let me introduce the lady who'll be working with you on your short game: Lee Ofsted, one of the most glamorous, up-and-coming stars of the WPGL. As you'll soon find out, Lee is more than a pretty face. She has plenty to show you about getting up on the green . . . and off again . . . in the fewest possible strokes. Lee, care to stand up and say a few words at this point?"

She gulped. Why the heck hadn't Jackie warned her? Here they all were, turning brightly toward her, as if they expected more of the same smooth blarney. She got up, her throat dry, searching a mind abruptly empty for something witty to say, something clever. *Duh . . . um . . .*

"It's a pleasure to be here," she mumbled. "I'm really looking forward to working with you."

They waited expectantly for more. She licked dry lips. "With each and every one of you," she said quickly, and sat down.

Peg leaned toward her. "That was just fine," she said kindly, which didn't help.

"Well," Jackie said, rubbing his hands together, "that takes care of the preliminaries. And now it's . . ." He spread his arms palms-out. "*Showtime!*"

Chapter 5

"Showtime" was putting it mildly. It was more like one-man-circus time. Jackie started off with a bang, wowing his audience with a spirited performance that even Lee found entertaining.

"I know you've all heard," he said, standing up to a row of golf balls with a graphite-shafted Jackie Piper Stroke-Cutter 3-iron, "that a firm, straight left arm is the key to an effective golf swing. Well . . ."

And with that he swung at the ball with a left arm about as firm as a boiled egg noodle. The ball took off, true as an arrow, soaring white against the blue sky—was there anything in all this world as beautiful and eye-catching as an arcing, well-struck golf ball against a brilliant sky?—and finally came down smack in the center of the practice range a good two hundred yards away.

Most of his audience laughed and clapped. Lee clapped along with them.

Jackie looked puzzled. "What do you know, I guess maybe the elbow isn't the main thing after all. He stroked his chin, pretending to be at a loss. "*I* know! I read it in a book somewhere. The main thing is to get that body weight effectively transferred from the right foot to the left foot, right?"

"Right," a few people said, going along with him.

Jackie stepped up to the next ball, took his normal address position, then lifted his right foot completely up in the air so that he was balancing on his left leg alone. The club swung back, swished gracefully forward . . .

Whack. Two hundred yards.

"Yeah, sure," laughed a meaty man in his mid-forties with a ruddy, broken-veined drinker's face and an abundance of Hollywood-mogul jewelry—pinkie rings, gold chain around the neck, chunks of diamond glittering on his chain-link gold watch band—"but that's because you were standing on your *left* foot, the foot you transfer your weight *to.*"

"You could be right," Jackie agreed.

"You *know* I'm right, pal. Let's see you try it standing on your right foot."

"Oh, good idea!" Jackie said, and did.

Whack. Two hundred yards.

There was a sprinkle of applause, and a copper-haired woman two seats down from the meaty man said to him in a laughing stage whisper: "On the other hand, it could be that you're wrong."

"Ho, ho," he said.

"Hm, do you suppose it might have something to do with keeping your eye on the ball?" Jackie wondered. "I'm sure I heard that somewhere too." Ostentatiously he squeezed his eyes shut, twisted his neck so that he was facing backward for good measure, and swung.

Whack.

And on it went. He swung with his hands reversed, right above left, he swung without using his right hand at all, he swung in apparent slow motion.

Whack. Whack. Whack.

It was fun, but Lee had seen most of it before, from one trick golfer or another, and it had long ago ceased to amaze—except to make her wonder why these tricksters, if they were so proficient, never managed to succeed on the pro tour. But really, she knew the answer to that: the physical skills were necessary but nowhere near sufficient to make it in the big time. It took grinding determination, it took the discipline to subordinate everything else in your life to getting a 1.7" dimpled ball into a 4.25" metal cup in the fewest possible strokes, it took the tenacity to trudge out to the range and hit a dozen buckets of balls after a bone-wearying day in competition, it took the not-so-common ability to stay loose under fantastic pressure, it took the willingness to spend most of your life among strangers, in strange towns—a new one every week—living out of suitcases, doing your laundry in Laundromats and motel sinks, swallowing one disappointment after another (even the greatest golfers won only a small fraction of their tournaments), and living on hope.

In short, it helped a lot to be crazy, and Jackie Piper didn't seem crazy.

Lee, sitting next to Peg at one end of the row, used the time to study the people who were going to be in her charge for the next few days. Even without their name tags, they would have been easy to tell apart from Peg's descriptions on the trip from the airport.

The bland, abstracted man with the graying mustache, the straw hat, the plus fours, and the brown-and-white wing-tip golf shoes—in 1940 he would have been the height of fashion—was Stuart Chappell, founder and president of SRS. Kindly, pleasant, and utterly unremarkable, it was impossible to imagine him as ever having been an adventurous young salvage diver, try as Lee might. He had stood up to make a few rambling introductory remarks before Jackie had begun, and Lee had tried to pay attention but he quickly left her behind when he wandered vaguely off into the New Age with "value-based decision-making," "empowerment utilization," and "multifunctional work teams." A glance at the others told her that she wasn't the only one having trouble tracking. Even Peg looked a little lost.

Since then Stuart had had little to say, preferring to sit quietly, his hands loosely clasped over a neat little paunch, his face turned up to the sun, and his eyes closed most of the time, so at peace that he might have been asleep. Or maybe he was asleep, who could tell? But as Peg had said, he seemed like a pretty good egg, and Lee had taken an early liking to him. He was, after all, her benefactor, since he was paying Jackie and Jackie was paying her. *Thank you, Mr. Chappell,* she thought gratefully.

Sitting beside him was a brusque, hard-faced woman, fifteen or twenty years his junior and wearing a chicly understated gray-and-white golf outfit that had to have cost more than Lee's clothing allotment for the year. That would be Stuart's wife, Darlene, the Tough Cookie, the Grand Czarina. Darlene had probably been sveltely beautiful only a few years ago, but she was one of those women whom age was not treating gently. Forty at most, and well preserved—or rather, well maintained—her body, though still athletic, was beginning to get boxy now, and she had had a face-lift or two that hadn't worked out as intended, leaving her with tight, lizardy lips and narrow, mean, almost lidless eyes.

Lee had already noticed those eyes openly checking her over in a manner that didn't exactly suggest they were on the brink of a burgeoning friendship, and she had decided Peg was right: Darlene Chappell was not someone on whose wrong side it would be a good idea to get.

And the meaty guy with the red nose, the one with the pinkie rings and the glittery, gold-and-diamonds wristwatch, was Bert

Balboni, in charge of sales and marketing. "If ever a guy looked like your glad-handing, laugh-a-minute, let's-have-one-for-the-road supersalesman," Peg had said, "that's Bert." The description fitted him to a tee.

Thanks to Peg's lively descriptions, Lee also recognized the copper-haired woman as SRS's chief financial officer, Ginny Briggs. "You know what happens to a cat when it strolls around a corner and suddenly comes face-to-face with a dog?" Peg had asked. "That's Ginny."

Lee hadn't been sure of what she'd meant at the time, but she understood now. Ginny Briggs, in her mid-thirties, was a petitely chunky, fresh-faced woman who seemed to have a lot going for her, but whose outstanding feature was surely her hair. There was no missing that: a kinky sunburst of wiry copper strands that sprang straight off her scalp, the way a cartoon character's hair does when he sticks his finger in an electrical socket. You could practically hear the *sproing-g-g*.

At thirty-five Ginny was the youngest member of the executive staff and the only woman, and despite her chipper—perhaps overly chipper—energetic manner, Lee had the impression that she was still struggling to find her place among these big, male fish.

"You'll be happy to learn," Jackie said when the last of a dozen balls had rocketed off his clubhead (he was sitting on a folding chair at the time), "that there's a point to all these little tricks. Would anybody like to guess what it is?"

"Sure," said a jolly, bespectacled fireplug of a man with rolls of chin fat, a head as bald as an ostrich egg, and a dead cigar wedged in the corner of his mouth. This was Frank Wishniak, chief consulting engineer and at sixty-one the oldest of the group and the only one who had been with Stuart from the beginning. The "consulting engineer" title was strictly honorary; in actuality Frank had never graduated from high school. He had been working in a New London shipyard as a welder-diver when Stuart had hired him as his very first employee and right-hand man. He had been there ever since: more than twenty-five years, moving up in rank as Stuart's business grew.

A loyal pal, Stuart Chappell.

"I understand everything now," Frank was saying with a gargly laugh. "How could I not see it before? The whole key is to hit the ball with your eyes closed while you're sitting in a chair facing the wrong way. Right?" He jiggled with silent laughter from his wattles to his white, hairless, bowling-ball calves.

"Egg-*zack*-ly!" Jackie said, chortling along with him. "However, I must report that under appendix four, paragraph sixteen, subparagraph twenty-four, section three (a) of the USGA guidelines, the use of chairs on the tee has recently been ruled illegal."

He slipped the iron into his bag and turned relatively sober, slowing down to only a few hundred words a minute. The reason he could fool around the way he had with the various parts of the swing, he explained, was that a golf swing was something different from the simple sum of its parts.

"What's the most beautiful, most graceful animal there is?" he asked. "How about a racehorse? Well, suppose you wanted to figure out how it moved like that, so you dissected it and laid it all out on a big table: muscles, bones, ligaments, blood vessels, nerves, the works. Would you know its secret? Nope, you'd have bits and snippets of horse, sure . . . but you wouldn't have any *horse*. That's how it is with the golf swing; to be effective it has to be one piece, a *whole*, not a collection of little jogs and turns and twists that no one can possibly keep in mind during the swing anyway."

Lee nodded. She'd heard this part of the pitch before, on his infomercials, and she couldn't argue with it.

"So then how," Jackie continued, returning to his cheerful, rapid-fire patter, "do you develop a smooth, effective, one-piece swing that gives you both distance and accuracy? That's the crucial question, isn't it?"

"Is it ever," Peg murmured dolefully.

Was it ever, Lee thought. Golf addicts like Peg plunked down over a billion dollars a year for books and lessons and gadgets in the hunt for the definitive answer.

To Lee's knowledge, nobody had found it yet; not a definitive one anyway.

"And the answer is . . ." Jackie said.

Imaging, Lee said silently to herself.

"Imaging!" Jackie shouted. "Creating an image that you can easily keep in your mind that prompts your body to automatically do the right thing!"

Well, that was where Lee parted company with him. She didn't have the answer either, but she was pretty sure that it wasn't standing in a barrel, real or imaginary. Still, as he'd said, he was just trying to make a living here, and if otherwise sane people couldn't wait to shell out good money for such things, who was she to object?

Jackie continued on this subject for some time, not failing to call frequent attention to the complete line of Stroke-Cutter practice aids that would be available for their inspection and purchase—at 15 percent off list price—throughout the week, until at last the man on Stuart Chappell's other side—Malcolm Labrecque, the newly anointed executive vice-president—raised a forefinger.

"I don't like to interrupt, but if we're going to work on individual swing diagnosis, hadn't we better get started? It's already"—he tapped the face of his digital watch—"three minutes after eleven."

Jackie staggered. "Omigod, eleven-oh-*three*! I'm three minutes over!" He smacked himself vigorously on the cheek, winced, and shook himself. "Thanks, Malcolm, I needed that! Whew. Sometimes I get so carried away by my own brilliance I lose all track of time. I tell you what, Malcolm. Whenever that happens, you are hereby authorized to keep me in line."

Others laughed, but Malcolm didn't see what was funny. "When *we're* at work we're expected to accomplish our objectives within specified time parameters. I really don't see why we shouldn't demand the same from you."

"Ooo," said Jackie, pretending to pull a spear from his chest. "Say, does anybody know how to staunch arterial bleeding?"

Ichabod Crane. That was who Malcolm Labrecque reminded Lee of. Not yet out of his thirties, but already stoop-shouldered, with a vaguely moth-eaten look and a meager, miserly face— what her mother used to call a lemon-sucker's face—he looked uncomfortable and out of place here in the sunny outdoors in his brand-new golf clothes. He would have seemed more at home, she thought, in some dim, gaslit office, sitting on a bookkeeper's high stool and wearing a green eyeshade. On the drive from the airport, Peg had said that despite his fusty appearance it was Malcolm's brilliant organizational and networking strategies that had put SRS on the map. Even Stuart had admitted as much.

Maybe so, but he sure wasn't going to be any fun to work for. Not if this was a sign of his managerial approach to come.

"All right, then, everybody, that's it for general swing instruction today!" Jackie clapped his hands together and gestured at the line of practice tees, behind which were wire racks holding the participants' golf bags at the ready. "To your battle stations!

Gentlemen and ladies, choose your weapons—in this case your pitching wedges—and prepare yourselves to be inducted into the mysteries of the approach game. I now deliver you into the capable hands of my erstwhile colleague, famous throughout the golfing world for the brilliance of her play and her mastery of the short game . . . Lee Ofsted!"

Lee got to her feet and grinned weakly. *Sheesh*, she thought.

Chapter 6

Lee's teaching session wasn't as hard to get through as she'd feared. She kept it simple, didn't even try to be funny, and tried to adapt her presentation to their individual problems. And like golfers everywhere they each had plenty of individual problems.

Bulbous, no-necked Frank Wishniak, with his dead cigar, big belly, and quivering jowls, had a golf swing that belonged on *The World's Funniest Videos*, a flapping, flailing, amazing spasm that made him look like a man fending off a cloud of hornets. Absolutely everything was wrong with it; Lee couldn't think where to start.

But the bluff, optimistic Frank couldn't have been more upbeat. "Listen, I've been thinking about increasing my upper-body rotation on my backswing," he told her. "To flatten the in-to-out arc?" He looked at her as if he'd hit at last on the secret of playing scratch golf. "What do you think? Would it be a good idea?"

Lee thought it over and replied with the full conviction of her native honesty. "It couldn't hurt," she said.

Stuart Chappell, on the other hand, was one of those golfers who are so sure they're going to mishit the ball that they approach every shot, even practice swings, with an air of resigned melancholy.

With reason. Stuart couldn't seem to get rid of what was surely the most extreme pause she had ever seen at the top of a backswing. He would take the club back a little too fast, but no worse than a lot of golfers did. But then, just as he started to bring it down, there would be this amazing hitch, as if he'd hooked the club on an invisible clothesline. And from there— once he'd gotten it unhooked—disaster followed inevitably, with arms, legs, hands, and hips all going off in their own unhelpful directions.

"What do you think?" he asked with his bemused smile. "Is there any hope?"

"Well, there is some room for improvement," she said, continuing her policy of tactful honesty.

In fact, she was able to help him a little by getting him to put the ball farther back in his stance, so that the club made contact with it every now and then. The improvement was modest, to say the least, but Stuart was grateful and Lee began to think that maybe she was pretty good at this after all.

Ginny Briggs, who had only played two or three times before, was a willing student, the most determined of them all to improve her game, and although she had an aptitude for it, her very determination got in her way. She wrapped her fingers around the grip like grim death, so that the tendons stood out like straws on the backs of her hands. Lee tried some of Jackie's imaging techniques to get her to relax: "Imagine that you're holding a child's hand. Or better yet, pretend that you're holding a small, frightened bird; you don't want it to fly away, but you don't want to hurt it either."

Imaging didn't help. On Ginny's next swing, the loosely grasped club went pinwheeling out of her hand, missing Stuart's nose by two feet and coming to rest about sixty yards down the range.

"How about that?" Ginny said ruefully. "I can throw the club farther than I can hit the ball."

"Still," Lee said, accentuating the positive, "it does seem you're able to relax your grip when you try."

"Great. Now all I have to do is find a happy medium."

At first Malcolm Labrecque puzzled Lee. Indifferent to and even resentful of her suggestions, restless, preoccupied, he gave every indication of wishing himself anywhere but there.

"Forgive me," she finally said, "but you don't really seem all that interested in golf."

"I hate golf. It's the most flagrant consumer of priority hours known to man."

She lowered the wedge she'd been using to demonstrate. "You hate—then why are you here?"

"Because Stuart told us to be here."

"Oh," she said.

He looked her pointedly in the eye. "Just don't expect me to actually *play*."

"No," said Lee, "I certainly won't."

There was only one first-rate golfer in the group, and that was Bert Balboni, which didn't surprise Lee. He was a type often found around golf and country clubs, on the course and at the bar in about equal measure. A relaxed, deft swing—he'd had plenty of lessons, that was clear—and a powerful if overweight physique contributed to his respectable 6-handicap. There really wasn't much that Lee could show him about short-game basics, but she was able to give him some points on his pitch-and-run, one of the more difficult shots to execute well, and he accepted her help in his teasing, boozy way. Lee couldn't tell if all the laid-back joshing came naturally or if he went around doing a perpetual but not overly successful Dean Martin imitation. Whichever, the Scotch on his breath, discernible through an eye-watering haze of aftershave and breath freshener, was real enough.

By the end of the morning, Lee was feeling pretty good. She was earning her pay, she was being fairly well received, and she actually seemed to be helping those who wanted help. (Well, Frank was beyond help but he was having a good time.) The fly in the ointment was Darlene.

"Now, wait a minute," she said when Lee had barely gotten started, "if we open our stance the way you're telling us to, we'd be stepping out of the barrel."

"If so," Lee answered pleasantly, "maybe when you're using a wedge you should just imagine a bigger barrel."

"Oh, really?" Darlene said in her blunt, challenging way, with not a hint of an answering smile. "Nobody told me they came in sizes."

And so it went. Darlene had a natural tendency to be contrary, to complain, and she indulged it frequently. She also had a natural ability to get under Lee's skin. Lee was having a hard time telling if she was as shrewd and nasty as everyone seemed to think, or merely dumb and nasty. Either way, it was clear that she was going to be the cross that Lee would have to bear all week. But at a thousand dollars a day she didn't expect to have any trouble summoning up the necessary patience and good humor.

And there were other benefits as well. Lunch, served under a striped awning on the Mooncussers' terrace, was a luscious, amply portioned, rosy-pink lobster salad with tarragon-mayonnaise dressing. Ah, yes, she thought, plumping herself and her well-filled plate down next to Peg, she would bear up just fine.

"What do you think?" Peg asked. "How's it going so far?"

Lee stuck her fork into a tender nugget of lobster tail and grinned at her friend. "Piece of cake, Peggy, my girl. Piece of cake."

*   *   *

Back at Quonochaugachaug for the afternoon round, Jackie divided the attendees into two threesomes: Stuart, Bert, and Peg in one, and Darlene, Ginny, and Frank in the other. Malcolm, true to his word, had remained at the inn.

Lee, in a charitable mood brought on by positive thinking and lobster salad, decided that it was partially her own fault that she'd gotten off on the wrong foot with Darlene, and in hopes of making amends, offered to go around with Darlene's group. It was, after all, only nine holes, and short ones at that, and there would be two other people along to keep things friendly.

What could happen?

Chapter 7

Frank Wishniak cupped both hands over his mouth. "Fore!" he bellowed toward the far end of the fairway, where Stuart Chappell was just finishing up on the green. Inasmuch as the far end of the fairway was some two hundred twenty yards away, and Frank's longest drive so far had been eighty-five yards (including bounces), it seemed to Lee that he was being somewhat needlessly careful. But that, she was learning, was Frank for you—not a man to have his optimism dimmed by a few little failures.

"Frank," she said mildly, "I think you can probably go ahead and swing. I don't think Stu's in very much danger."

"You never know," Frank said. "I feel *good.* I could really belt this one."

Ginny laughed. "Frank, I hate to tell you this, but you're living in a fantasy world here."

Frank's big belly jiggled with a soundless chuckle. "Young lady, if I didn't have a fantasy life I wouldn't have a life."

A huge, impatient sigh came from Darlene. "Could we get on with it, please? I'm going to forget where my ball is."

Frank grumbled good-naturedly, tugged at the crumpled fisherman's hat he wore to protect his bald head from the sun, and set himself over the ball. "Just you watch," he said, working the dead cigar stub into the corner of his mouth and waggling himself into position. "Just you watch. Here we go, now."

Frank was one of those players who talk themselves through their swings, a habit capable of driving many fellow golfers around the bend. Unfortunately Lee was one of them, but today she found it easy to keep her mind tranquil and her spirits high by silently repeating a simple, relaxing mantra whenever he was at the tee: "A thousand dollars a day, a thousand dollars a day . . ."

"Okay, now," Frank told himself, "*this* is going to be good." Another whole-body waggle. "Toes lined up . . . check. V's pointing at the right shoulder . . . check. Elbows close in . . ."

"*This* is going to take forever," Darlene muttered in that flat, challenging voice of hers. "I'm going to forget where my ball is."

". . . check," continued an unperturbed Frank. "Head down . . . check. Weight distributed . . . check. And now for the swing."

"God be praised," said Darlene.

As usual, Frank practically turned himself inside out with that lurching swing of his, sending the ball skittering twenty yards through grass directly to his right. A worm-burner.

"Mulligan!" he yelled immediately, the duffer's appeal for a free shot when the first one has been boggled. Among friends, informal etiquette usually allowed for one per round, the philosophy being that everybody was entitled to one mistake. This was Frank's third of the day. And it was only the fourth hole.

Darlene was steaming. "This is impossible! We're going to be here all damn day. On *this* hole, I mean! I'm going to go find my ball." And off she stomped toward the left rough as Frank pulled a ball from his pocket, set it just so on the tee, and happily started all over again. "Toes lined up . . ."

Darlene had teed off a couple of minutes before, hitting her usual shot, a solid, generally competent drive, but with a tendency to tail off to the left over its last seventy or eighty yards. In other words, a hook. On the previous hole Lee had tactfully suggested that she might want to open her stance and weaken her grip a little to correct it, but Darlene, unsurprisingly, had resisted help and Lee had let it drop, concentrating instead on Frank and Ginny, who wanted (and needed) all the help they could get.

But this hook had been a total disaster, starting off a little to the right of center, then curving across the entire breadth of the fairway and into the rough, a tangle of black alder and bayberry bushes, where it had ricocheted off one of the island's few trees and rocketed backward thirty or forty yards before being swallowed up by the foliage.

"Oh, gosh," Ginny said, watching Darlene plunge into the tangle, "look at that, she *did* forget where her ball is."

"No, she just didn't see it hit the tree and bounce back," Lee said. "Well, she's sure never going to find it where she is. I'll go help her. It's pretty much on the way to my ball anyway."

"No hurry," Ginny said with a sigh, gesturing at the statuelike figure concentrating so intently over the ball. "We'll be here a while yet."

"Weight distributed . . ." Frank was saying.

*   *   *

Lee strode loosely along the edge of the fairway, easily lugging her lightweight practice bag with a mere six clubs in it. It had been a couple of days since she'd had any exercise, and it did her good to get her legs going, and feel the clean, cool salt air flowing over her face, and hear the clubs chinking rhythmically on her shoulder. So much so that she lost track of where she was heading and thought she might have overshot the area of rough into which Darlene had disappeared.

She stopped and called. "Darlene? Your ball's back a ways." No answer; just the soft rustle of leaves. "Darlene?"

For no reason she could name, the hairs on the back of her neck rose. A shivery tingle curled down the middle of her back. "Darlene? Are you all right?"

She took a club from the bag, put the bag down, and began to retrace her steps along the edge of the rough, peering into dark bushes, pushing branches aside with the club. "Darlene?"

At a sudden, alarmingly close explosion of sound she caught her breath and stiffened. Something was in there, something frenzied, something big. Branches were splintering, hooves— *hooves?*—were thrashing. She froze, her heart in her throat, not knowing which way to run even if she'd been able to move, and clutching the club in both hands with a grip that outdid Ginny's. Good gosh, what kind of animals did they have here? Wild boar? Moose? *Rhinoceros?*

None of the above. What burst out of the bush directly in front of her was an agitated, red-faced Darlene Chappell in mid-bleat.

"Halp! H—"

At which point she caught her toe on a breadbox-sized boulder, one of the scattered remnants of the old stone wall that had once run along the edge of the fairway. *"Yi—!"*

"Watch—" cried Lee too late, holding up both hands but unable to ward off the careening Darlene. An instant later they were sprawled on the grass staring at each other.

"Darlene—what—"

"Lee!" the flabbergasted Darlene yelped. "I . . . thank God . . ." She looked frantically back at the bushes. "He . . . he tried . . . he was . . ."

"*Who?*" Lee shrieked back, staring, understandably bug-eyed, into the foliage as well.

The answer provided itself. Clumping out of the brush with a ferocious churning of leaves and branches came a man the size (and shape) of a heavy-duty home freezer, who promptly ran into the same rock that Darlene had, was catapulted into a squealing somersault ("*Whoowhoowhoo!*"), and landed with a thunderous "*Whuff!*" on the seat of his pants, his eyes squeezed shut.

When he opened them he was patently astounded. "Huh . . . ?"

If Lee hadn't been frightened half out of her wits she would have laughed. There the three of them were in the grass, after all, sitting on their fannies in a circle, close enough to share a bowl of chips and dip if one had been there, and goggling at each other, all of them obviously dumbfounded. The hulking newcomer wore Bermudas and a tank-top shirt that revealed a pale, hairless chest and freckled, blubbery, pink-splotched shoulders. He was wearing about the worst wig she'd ever seen, a jet-black, plastic-fibered thing that looked as if it had come from the drugstore Halloween racks and that now sat askew on his head. Under it Lee could see some close-cropped, almost colorless hair. His jaw was heavy, his nose flattened, his expression definitely of the dim-bulb variety. He looked, Lee thought, an awful lot like one of the Three Stooges, the one that was always getting poked in the eye by the guy with the pageboy.

He straightened the wig clumsily, almost prissily. "Let's have no trouble, ladies. I don't want to hurt anyone." Assuming that he was trying to cow them, his high-pitched, nervous voice didn't help any. He even sounded like Moe, or Shemp, or whichever one it was.

Darlene and Lee exchanged a glance. There was no weapon in evidence, no gun, no knife. If they both scrambled to their feet and ran, what could he do?

But he was quicker than he looked, and more formidable. Before they could move, one huge, blunt-fingered hand darted out to clamp onto Darlene's wrist. She hammered ineffectually at it with her other fist. "You bastard, let me go! What do you want?"

He stood up, pulling her roughly to her feet, and shook her arm hard, just once. The tremor went through her whole body, like a ripple in a snapped whip. It was enough to quiet her down at once. "All right—okay—don't hurt me," she said quickly. She sounded scared to death.

Lee didn't blame her; she would have been scared to death too. She was more than scared enough as it was. The guy might look like a bonehead, but he was big, and he was strong, and he was fast. Who knew what he wanted, what he would do? She had jumped up and backed away a few steps while he was manhandling Darlene, just enough to get out of range of his free hand. She had never let go of the club, and now, to her amazement, she found herself brandishing it at him, blocking his way back into the brush, into which he was obviously intending to haul Darlene.

"You let her go right now," Lee said, but it was about all she could do to get the words out. There seemed to be no air in her lungs; her arms were watery; her legs didn't seem to be there at all. "I—I warn you, I'll use this if I have to."

Unfortunately it was somewhat lacking in conviction. Moreover, the club was a wedge and not one of her heavy-duty long irons, and it seemed about as threatening as a matchstick against this bruiser, who was showing no signs of alarm. His only reaction was to change his grip on Darlene, getting the crook of his arm around her neck like a vise. Darlene grew even more still. Her hands tugged weakly at his ham-shaped forearm, but she was no longer really struggling. Her eyes, on Lee the whole time, were enormous and pleading.

"I gotta go now, lady," the man told Lee almost apologetically, "so you better get out of my way. I got no quarrel with you. I want her, that's all."

"You *want* her!" Lee echoed stupidly. "For what?"

The man stared at her. "Well, not for what you're thinking!" he exclaimed with every indication of offended propriety, and once again Lee almost laughed.

At that moment Darlene bit his arm, and when he yelped Lee took the opportunity to swing the wedge at him. He flung up his hand and batted it harmlessly aside, but in so doing he let go of Darlene, and now the Tough Cookie showed her mettle. She was all over him, an avenging Fury, kicking, screaming, cursing, and, when anything came within reach, biting.

The big man, more annoyed than inconvenienced by all this, raised his hand to cuff her, but an energized Lee managed to hook it out of the way with the head of the club and then came charging in, ducking under his arm and butting him in the ribs with her head, bringing another soul-satisfying *whuff*. Darlene was on his right, giving it her all, Lee on his left, doing the same. They were like a couple of yipping foxes worrying a big, slow, confused bear.

"Ow!" he squawked. "*Ow*, dammit!" He swatted ineffectually at them.

"Hey you, hey, cut that out! What's going on there?"

And here came Ginny running up the fairway toward them. Straggling behind her, gasping and pop-eyed—it was he who had shouted—but galumphing bravely along all the same, was Frank Wishniak, with fire in his eyes.

"Oh, for God's sake, can you believe this?" the big man muttered disgustedly. "What is this, a party or something?"

Like a huge dog just out of the water, he shook his body ponderously, spilling Lee and Darlene onto the grass, then clapped one hand onto the retilted wig, turned, and went crashing back through the brush, grousing audibly to himself.

The two women scrambled to their feet, glanced at one another again, and without exchanging a word, chased after him. They heard a car door slam while they were still in the rough and ran even harder, but by the time they came out of the bushes onto the quiet country road that bordered the course he was already gunning the engine of a dusty maroon van. The tires spun, squealed, and caught; the van lurched forward in a spray of gravel.

"Get the license!" Darlene yelled over the noise, but Lee had something else in mind. She still had the wedge, and running alongside the accelerating vehicle, acting on impulse, she thrust it, clubhead first, into the spinning rear right wheel, hoping that it might stick in there and jam something.

Stick it did, but not jam. The club was ripped out of her hand and went *whap-whapping* down the road, caught in the wheel, one *whap* per rotation. On the fourth one, it came free. In pieces. The grip split and was torn away. The shaft collapsed into a lopsided V. The head broke off and flew into the bushes.

Her new wedge. Her graphite-shafted, $180 Cobra 60-degree lob wedge that she hadn't even used in a tournament yet, that she had brought along just so she could practice with it.

"Did you get the number?" Darlene asked.

"What? No." Her brand-new wedge! Why couldn't it have been that ancient mallet-putter she was thinking of getting rid of?

"Damn," Darlene said, and then more vigorously: "Damn!" She rubbed her neck and grimaced.

"Darlene, are you all right?" Lee asked. She was feeling almost fond of the Grand Czarina, the fondness of one brave and victorious battle comrade for another. And Darlene *had* been brave. It would have been easy for her to simply run like hell when he had let go of her after Lee had swung the club at him. Instead, she had stayed right there with Lee, lighting into him like a one-woman army.

Darlene continued to knead the skin at the base of her skull. "No, I'm not all right," she said with a disagreeable scowl. "My neck's killing me. It took you long enough to *do* something. I thought you were just going to stand there and let him choke the life out of me."

You're welcome, Lee thought grumpily. Goodbye, world's shortest friendship.

"Although I suppose I should be thankful for what you did do," the older woman allowed in a Darlenish version of gratitude. She worked her head from side to side. "Oh, don't look so down in the mouth, Lee, I'm fine."

"Great, I'm glad to hear it," Lee said, taking one last, lingering look at the wrecked shaft lying on the verge of the road like so much discarded trash, before they turned to meet the panting, onrushing Ginny and Frank.

Chapter 8

"That it?" asked one-third of the New Shoreham police department, in the person of Chief Arnold Tolliver. The pipe-smoking Chief Tolliver, along with one sergeant and one corporal, constituted the official, year-round police presence on Block Island, which was still technically on the books as the Town of New Shoreham, the name bestowed by the first white settlers, refugees from the Massachusetts Bay Colony, in 1672.

"That's about it, I think," Lee said. "I just wish I'd gotten the license plate number."

"Description helps," the chief said. He finished making the last of his notes, slipped the pad into the pocket of his short-sleeved sport shirt, and relit his stubby, metal-stemmed pipe for about the tenth time. "It's Curly, by the way—that's the one you're thinking of. Curly, Moe, and Larry."

That was more than anything else she'd been able to get out of him up to now. Chief Tolliver was not what you would call loquacious. If he had opinions, and she had no doubt that he did, he kept them strictly to himself. Although he had the look of a veteran big-city cop—beefy, grizzled, hard-bitten—he spoke with an easy-to-listen-to rural drawl and appeared to approach life with a philosophy that was equal parts there's-nothing-new-under-the-sun and what-will-be-will-be. If they ever needed any-one to fill in for Andy Griffith as police chief of Mayberry, Arnold Tolliver was their man.

He buttoned his pocket, got the pipe drawing, and looked ap-praisingly around him. "Nice place."

Lee nodded her agreement. They were on the sloping back lawn of the inn, overlooking the Sound, sitting in white wrought-iron chairs with a frosted pitcher of mango tea on the glass-topped table next to them. To their right, under a sky muted with high, gauzy clouds, the lawn swept prettily down to-ward a reed-bordered pond with a weathered swimming dock in it, and a pristine beach of white sand just beyond. To the left, at the edge of the flagstone terrace, a portable bar had been rolled out and the female bartender—the same woman who had been waiting tables that morning—was expertly dispensing booze and soft drinks. Given the unexpected excitement of the after-noon's events, the cocktail hour had gotten under way early, and the SRS crowd, mostly on their second drinks by now, were gathered in twos and threes on lawn and terrace in a giddy, al-most jolly mood. Only the center of attention, Darlene herself, was absent, having grabbed a double gin and water after her ses-sion with Chief Tolliver a few minutes earlier and stomped off with it to unkink in the whirlpool tub.

A quiet whinny of laughter from Stuart Chappell made Lee and the chief turn around. Stuart was standing on the terrace a few yards away with Benny Trotter and Peg. He was reading a sheet of paper with a look of amused incredulity in his pale eyes. "Unbelievable. Chief Tolliver, I think you'll be interested in this."

Softly chortling, he headed for Lee and the chief. Peg, as candidly, joyfully nosy as anyone Lee had ever met, sauntered right along with him. After a moment's hesitation, so did Benny.

"Got something there, Mr. Chappell?" Chief Tolliver asked from his chair.

"Indeed I do." He rattled the paper, cleared his throat somewhat theatrically, and began to read in his pleasant, slightly nasal voice:

"Stuart Chappell:
We have your wife. If you want to see her alive again—

Tolliver held his hand out. "Well, now, I think you'd better let—"

But Stuart snatched the sheet away almost playfully, retreated a couple of steps, and continued to read.

"—it will cost you $650,993. Make immediate arrangements to have the money available for electronic transfer. We will contact you shortly. Do not leave the island. Do not involve the police or we will put her out of her misery. This is no joke. We mean everything we say."

Having finished, he handed over the typewritten sheet along with a torn envelope that had "Mr. Stuart Chappell" typed on the front. Nothing else. And no stamp.

"Say," Benny exclaimed suddenly. "They must have sent that note before they ever tried to get her!"

Stuart smiled tolerantly at him. "Do you know, Benny, that very same thought had passed through my mind. Do you think we might be dealing with a slight case of overconfidence here?"

"How'd you get this?" Tolliver asked, getting to his feet.

"In the mail."

"Pretty hard to get a letter in the mail without a stamp."

"Somebody must've put it in the lobby mailbox," Benny volunteered. "I just found it."

"Who has access to that?"

Benny shrugged, his bright blue eyes round. "Anybody."

"Meaning anybody who's here now, isn't that so? The hotel's closed this week, isn't it, except for this group?"

"Not exactly," Benny said. "We're open to the public for lunch in the dining room—Stu and his people eat out here on the terrace. Had a crowd today too; ran out of oysters. Day-trippers are starting early this year."

Tolliver sighed. "I don't guess anyone saw anybody put anything in the box?" he said without much hope.

"I'll certainly ask."

By now most of the others had gathered round. "Mr. Chappell," Tolliver said, "why don't we go find ourselves someplace to talk?"

When everyone else had drifted away, Peg sat down next to Lee with her gin and tonic. "Are you going to get something to drink?"

"I'll stick with tea," Lee said, pouring herself a little more. "Pretty strange doings, huh?"

"I'll say. These people, whoever they are, give a whole new dimension to the word 'inept.' And how about that amount? Six hundred and fifty thousand something-something-something. What kind of ransom demand is that? It's weird."

"I know. Maybe they wanted it to buy something specific—a yacht or something—and that's what it costs."

"So? Why not just round it off to seven hundred thousand? Get a few deck chairs while they're at it."

Lee shook her head. "Don't ask me. Does Stuart really have that kind of money?"

"I would think so, yes. And by the way, what was he so all-fired merry about? He couldn't stop laughing."

"I don't know, he seemed closer to hysterical to me."

"No, that's just the way the man laughs. He was enjoying himself."

"Well, he got his wife back, didn't he, all in one piece?"

Peg looked at Lee over the rim of her glass, one eyebrow cocked. "And if *you* were Stuart Chappell and you got Darlene back after almost losing her, would you be chortling with joy?"

Lee laughed. "I see what you mean, but you know, there's no accounting for other people's taste in the opposite sex." But a moment later she couldn't help adding: "Or maybe he's just happy because he figures if they tried once, they're bound to try again, and maybe next time they'll succeed."

"Not if they don't have their act together any better than they did this time, they won't. Talk about losers. Did they do anything right?"

"Not much," Lee said thoughtfully. "You know, I was almost sorry for that plug-ugly out there on the course. He just—well, he looked the part all right, and he did his best, but he just didn't seem cut out for that line of work, if you know what I mean."

Peg smiled. "That line of work, as you call it, doesn't usually attract rocket scientists, you know. All right, go call Graham. You have time to do it before dinner."

Lee blinked at her. "How did you know I was going to call Graham?"

"Because you have that look on your face."

"Well, you're right," Lee said, wondering how many of her other thoughts were equally transparent. "He tried to get me this morning in Portland and left a message on my machine, so I guess I just had him on my mind and I—"

"Hey, what are you getting defensive about? I think it's sweet." She raised her glass in farewell. "Beat it. See you at dinner." And then, as Lee strode across the terrace: "And don't forget to say hi from me!"

*　　*　　*

She had flown up to her room without touching the stairs, or so it seemed to her, but the moment she closed the door behind her, sat down at the table in the sunlit bay window, and picked up the telephone to call him, she hesitated, seized with a crisis of confidence.

She'd been having a lot of them lately. Things had changed between the two of them since he'd quit the Carmel police department and gone into his globe-trotting business as a consultant. Or not so much between them, exactly, as around them. To put it in a nutshell, the tables had turned. In the old days, it was Graham who'd had to stay in one place and mark time while she was busy zipping around the glamorous pro tour, from Tucson, to Philadelphia, to Hartford, to Atlanta. But now it was Graham who was doing the glamorous zipping around. And forget Hartford and Atlanta; with him it was London and Paris. In the good old days—last year—she had laughed when he showed an occasional glimmer of insecurity about all the fascinating, irresistible sports stars and TV celebrities she was supposedly meeting (she wasn't), but she wasn't laughing now.

How long would it be before some beautiful, smart, successful corporate executive type realized just how neat he was and invited him out to a power lunch or something, and got her manicured, enameled hooks into him? Graham loved her; Lee didn't need Peg to tell her that, but he was also a wonderfully attractive, funny, patently decent guy, and he was on the loose, and—thanks to Lee's reservations in the past—there was no formal commitment between them.

That day in New Mexico seven months ago, when he had bowled her over by announcing that he was quitting the force and going into business as a consultant, she had sensed all morning that something important was coming, and she'd been petrified with indecision, certain that it was going to be an engagement ring. For months he'd been giving her subtle indications that he was more than ready to put their relationship on a more solid footing, and she'd been just as subtly letting him know that she preferred it the way it was, thank you.

It was funny, really. On the one hand, she was wildly in love with him, head over heels, and had been since almost the moment she'd met him. But on the other, she was fiercely protective of her fledgling golf career, of all the work and determination and sacrifice that had gone into it, and she feared that if she let him get too close, if she let *anyone* get too close, that strength, that passionate, single-minded resolve, would fritter away and be lost.

Without golf, her life would have been empty. She couldn't, wouldn't, give it up, not after all she'd put into it. But living without Graham . . . no, that was unthinkable too. She simply couldn't be without him, not anymore. And so, as he'd reached into the pocket of his jacket with that nervous, happy smile on his face, she'd sat there, dithering and miserable, unable to decide what her answer would be—*yes* was impossible, *no* was unimaginable . . .

So what does the guy do? Instead of a diamond ring he pulls out a snappy new cream-colored business card and hands it to her: *Countermeasure, Inc., Graham T. Sheldon, President*. She was so relieved she'd burst into giddy laughter, and even now she laughed, remembering.

How times change. The shoe was on the other foot now, and she was having a hard time remembering just what it was that was so objectionable about the idea of being engaged, particularly to someone like Graham. What had she been thinking of? How was a little more peace of mind on this highly important score supposed to ruin her golf game? She just hoped she hadn't discouraged him for good.

Well, live and learn. Maybe in her next life she'd be smarter. She sighed and dialed the lengthy string of numbers needed to reach his cellular phone in France.

"Hello?" The connection (did cell phones have "connections"?) wasn't good. His voice was thin and distant. And he sounded tired, worn. Well, that was hardly surprising. It was almost midnight in Paris.

"Graham—"

"Lee!" His weary voice came alive with a jolt. Even through four thousand miles of static and flutter his pleasure was transparent. For Lee, hearing it was like balm to an uneasy soul. Her insecurities, suddenly silly, melted away. She snuggled comfortably into the plush depths of the Victorian armchair, her feet tucked up under her.

"Lee, listen, I've wrapped up everything in Paris a day early. I'm finished here. And my meetings in Florence and Geneva—"

A few insecurities resurfaced, but only mildly.

"—don't start until next week, so all I have between now and next Monday is a two-day follow-up session in Toronto on Thursday and Friday. And you're not playing this week, right? So I was thinking maybe you could fly to Toronto tomorrow and meet me. We could have almost a whole week together. Or you could come to Paris for the week. I'd be away those two days in Canada, but we'd have all the rest of the time. Or if you want," he went on in an uncharacteristic flood of words, "you could come to Florence instead. Or London. Don't you want to see Europe? Don't worry about the money, believe me, I'm flush. Or maybe the Riviera, or the Amalfi Coast, or—"

"How about Rhode Island?"

"—or Capri, or, or—or—" He skidded to a halt. "How about what?"

"Rhode Island."

"What's in Rhode Island?" he asked after a lengthy pause.

"Me," she said, and explained.

"Well, sure," he said, a little deflated, when she'd finished. "It'll be wonderful to be with you anywhere. We'll have plenty of time for the exciting places later."

"Well, uh, to tell you the truth," she said, hesitating, "it's been pretty exciting here. Right up your alley, as a matter of fact. And I've sort of, um, been right in the middle of it, you might say."

"And what," he said darkly, "is that supposed to mean?"

Five minutes later she was undergoing her second grilling of the day, soon followed by an irate lecture; Graham at his police-manlike, imperious best. Didn't she know any better than to stand there and try to fight with that gorilla? Didn't she know that her best bet—for Darlene's safety as well as her own—would have been to run for help, making all the racket she could? Did she know how lucky she was she hadn't been hurt, even killed?

Lee mumbled one remorseful apology after another, all the while secretly basking in the warmth of this masterful show of concern. Every once in a while Graham got a little *too* master-ful—well, he was a man, after all; he couldn't help it—and Lee wasn't slow in telling him where to get off. But other times, when her spirits were low or she'd been through an unsettling experience, as she had today, it was wonderful to feel like a kid with this big, strong, commanding presence there to protect and take care of her. It was nothing she'd ever admit to Graham, of course, or to Peg, or to anyone else, but there it was all the same.

"I was only bruised a little," she murmured in a small voice, shamelessly and expertly milking the situation for all it was worth.

He came down off his high horse instantly. "Bruised! Lee, you didn't say—what do you mean, bruised? Are you all right? Why didn't you tell me—"

"Oh, it's nothing," she said quickly, warmed by his reaction but conscience-smitten too. "A tiny black-and-blue mark under one eye. I don't even know when it happened. My beautiful new wedge was the only real casualty."

A mistake, she realized too late; he was off and running again. "*That* was the dumbest thing of all," he told her angrily. "You might have done something useful if you'd done what Darlene said and gotten his license number."

"I know, but it just seemed—"

"And aside from maybe getting your arm torn out of its socket by the wheel, which you were lucky didn't happen, what were you going to do if it *had* stopped the car? He gets out, mad as hell now, makes a beeline for you—and then what?"

"Well—I guess I didn't plan that far ahead."

He started to say something else, but laughed instead; that lovely, easy laugh of his. "I love you, sweetheart. I'm just glad you're all right. What you did was really brave, but promise next time you'll think it through before you do anything impulsive."

"According to Chief Tolliver, there won't be any next time. He says the guy wouldn't try it again, not now anyway. He says he probably had a speedboat and was back on the mainland, or Long Island, or someplace, an hour after it happened."

"Fortunately I think your Chief Tolliver is right. Now let's talk about us. Is there an airport on the island?"

"Yes," she said, "but it's just a little one. I'm not even sure if it has commercial flights."

"That's okay, I'll get there. I'll be able to stay there tomorrow night and all day Wednesday, but I'll have to head for Toronto Wednesday night. Then I'll be back as early as I can on Saturday. Sound okay?"

She nodded eagerly, then remembered to say something: "Yes, yes!"

"Good. Call you in the morning, after I've chartered something from JFK."

"Chartered something? Graham, do you have any idea what that's going—" She stopped. "Oops, I keep forgetting I don't have a cop for a boyfriend anymore. I can't get used to your having money to throw away like that."

"Between you and me, neither can I," he laughed, "but I certainly hope to in time."

*   *   *

Lee had always been hard to drag out of sleep. She had slept through alarm clocks, telephones, and, on one memorable occasion, an earthquake measuring 5.2 on the Richter scale. But at 6:55 the next morning she was standing at the telephone, picking it up before its second chirp.

"Graham?"

"Did I wake you?"

"I don't know. Am I awake?" She yawned and scratched a mosquito bite on her side, under the oversized T-shirt (with "Go, Ducks!" across the front) that she slept in. She didn't remember hearing the phone ring, didn't remember stumbling blindly out of bed for it. All she knew was that she was tingling with excitement. "When will you be here?"

"Should be about six-thirty P.M. your time. I come into JFK at five, and an outfit called New England Airlines says they can have me at Block Island by six-thirty. Do you want to pick me up, or should I rent a car?"

"No, I'll pick you up!" She was wide awake now. "Oh, Graham, how wonderful. Am I really going to be seeing you today?"

"Wild horses couldn't keep me away," he said. "Bye, sweet."

"Bye . . . *wait!*"

But he was gone. Nothing but transatlantic static. "Damn," she said softly as she hung up. Six-thirty, she'd remembered, was smack in the middle of the social hour, to be followed by dinner at seven, both of which she was expected to attend. And Lee, despite a sometimes haphazard approach to life in general, took her professional commitments seriously. She was being well paid, she had been asked to be at the social functions, and she had agreed. That was that. Her spirits drooped, but she had no choice other than to call Graham back right now and tell him.

But even as she reached for her address book to find his number she felt herself wavering, and by the time she opened it she knew she had changed her mind. Surely, if she explained to Jackie that Graham was flying directly in from Paris just to see her, that she hadn't seen him in two months, and that he had to fly off again to Toronto the very next night, surely Jackie would tell her to take the evening off with his blessing. He would *want* her to, wouldn't he? He would feel bad about it if he were to find out that she had missed Graham's arrival just to schmooze with a bunch of people that would in all probability never miss her anyway. Of course he would.

So why was she so sheepish and mumbling when she asked

him about it at breakfast an hour later? But he reacted just the way she'd hoped.

"Sure, don't give it a thought," he said. "Have a good time. I'll hold the fort."

"I'll be there for every other night, I promise. It's just that this is so—"

He laughed. "Lee, relax, will you? It's no big deal, really. How's this: I am hereby *ordering* you to go meet your guy. Is that better?"

"Thanks, Jackie," she said with a smile, "that does make me feel better."

But still lousy.

Half an hour later, after she'd driven to the course with Peg and Ginny, she found a spot on the grass to do her morning stretching routine. Everybody else had gone to the shed to play with Jackie's Stroke-Cutter aids before the session got under way, so she was surprised to hear Stuart Chappell's quiet, pleasantly nasal voice at her side.

"Ah, me, I can't remember the last time I could touch my toes."

She got to her feet. "Good morning, Mr. Chappell."

She expected him to tell her to call him Stuart, but he didn't, which suited Lee. He was going on three times her age.

"Lee, I heard from Peg this morning that your young man is an expert on kidnapping." Lee noticed for the first time what sad eyes he had. Sad and gentle and dreamy, a dog's eyes. For the first time in years she found herself thinking of Jiggs, the long-suffering hybrid mutt the family had owned when she was a kid and, for a while when she was seven or eight, her best friend.

"Yes, he is," she said. "He's a security consultant."

"I'd like to get his views about what happened yesterday. Do you suppose he'd be willing to talk to me? I realize he'll be here on vacation, but I wouldn't expect to take much of his time and naturally I'd pay whatever his—"

"I'm sure he'd be glad to help if he can," Lee said.

"That's good." He paused with his hands behind his back, working his tongue around the inside of his cheek. "You see," he said softly, sadly, "I have some ideas about who's behind the abduction. The attempted abduction."

She stared at him. "Shouldn't you be talking to Chief Tolliver?"

"Well, it's a little awkward. I'd rather have your young man's advice first. Why don't you have him join us for drinks and dinner tonight? Then, if he has a minute or two afterward and wouldn't mind, I could pick his brains a bit."

Lee's face fell.

"Oh, I should have realized," Stuart said instantly. He was embarrassed. "You two must have other plans. Of course, forget that I asked. Tomorrow will be fine."

"But if it's important—"

"No, no, it will hold overnight. Sometime tomorrow, perhaps? Do you think he'd like to join us for breakfast, or would that be too early? Benny does put out the best breakfast on the island."

"I'm sure it'd be fine."

"Good. Then while the rest of you run off to the range, he and I can have our little chat."

"Mr. Chappell, I'm not comfortable with this. I don't think it's a good idea to wait—"

"Nonsense. Now let's talk about something *really* important while I have you alone for a while." He had his 8-iron with him and he took his stance. "Now, then. I've been giving some thought to what you said about delofting the club for chip shots . . ."

Chapter 9

"You look wonderful," Graham said.

"Even with my black eye?"

It was a little before 7 P.M. and they were sitting over coffee in the creamy evening sunlight, practically purring with the simple pleasure of being in each other's presence. They were on the elegant, otherwise deserted back terrace of the Hotel Manisses, the grande dame of Block Island's old inns, overlooking a quiet Victorian garden with a few pieces of white wrought-iron lawn furniture scattered about. The Manisses, a few hundred yards down Spring Street from the Mooncussers Inn, was where Graham had checked in after he and Lee had briefly discussed the pros (convenience, proximity to each other, sleeping arrangements) and cons (proximity to everybody else, lack of privacy) of his staying with her at the Mooncussers tonight. Graham was, if anything, a bit more old-fashioned than she was—even a little stuffy sometimes, if she was going to be completely honest—and it was he who had reluctantly concluded that for her to share a room with him during the training would have been unprofessional behavior. Lee, already sensitive about her professional behavior, had agreed.

On the other hand, it was also Graham who had suggested that when he had returned from Toronto and the program was over and the others had left, it would be fun to stay on for the weekend. With a chummier set of living arrangements.

"Oh, come on," he said now, "that's no black eye. You can hardly see it." Still, he reached tenderly out to touch the nickel-sized purplish bruise under her left eye with his fingertips, sending a little shiver up the back of her neck. "Besides, it gives you that certain *je ne sais quoi.*"

She laughed merrily, as if she knew what it meant. "You look terrific yourself." He did too, fit and tanned; all clean-cut planes and balanced, graceful lines, like a newspaper drawing for a men's clothing ad. "I just wish you'd warned me you were getting rid of the mustache. I never realized you had so much upper lip."

He fingered the bare expanse. "Want me to grow it back?"

"I don't know. Maybe. I was kind of used to it. I miss the tickle."

He smiled and leaned over to kiss her on the mouth, then to nuzzle her earlobe.

She laughed with her eyes closed. "On the other hand, I could get used to it this way too."

They had dinner in the Manisses' candlelit dining room, a long, elegant, extravagant meal of seafood chowder, smoked trout, and baked, stuffed lobster, then walked down Spring Street in the dark and along the hushed two-block stretch of Water Street that was the heart of Old Harbor, and finally onto Crescent Beach, the lovely, curving strip of white that had caught Lee's eye from the ferry. Even now, lit only by a veiled quarter-moon, the sand was pearly white. The water, except for faint, fleeting touches of phosphorescence where the low waves curled and quietly broke, was inky black. For a change, there was no wind at all.

They took off their shoes and walked hand in hand, lulled by the good food and half-hypnotized by the steady purling of the waves and the cool, grainy tickle of the sand against their bare feet. They went for long stretches of time hardly knowing what they talked about or whether they were talking at all, or even what they were thinking, aware of little more than a floating, lazy, delicious sense of happiness that Lee would have been content to have go on forever.

But after a while they began to come awake again, and return to the present, and the talk naturally turned to the kidnapping attempt.

"So how was your friend Darlene today?" Graham asked.

"Fine, why do you ask?"

"Because a lot of times after something like that a shock reaction sets in—weakness, apprehension, trembling. She showing any signs of that?"

Lee hooted. "Darlene? Are you kidding me? She was out there belting the ball this afternoon. She had a great round. Three birdies."

He stopped walking and frowned at her. "She was out on the course? The same course?"

"You mean it's dangerous for her? They might try again?"

"No, that's pretty unlikely at this point. But you'd think she'd want to stay close to the inn for a while for her own peace of mind; not be out in the open."

"You'd think so, yes, and that's exactly what Chief Tolliver told her to do, but you don't know the Grand Czarina. Wait'll you meet her."

Graham looked doubtful. "Do I have to?"

"Of course you do," Lee said firmly. "I can't wait to show you off, and other than Darlene, they're not bad at all. There are some real characters, believe me—"

"Oh, I believe you."

"And the thing is, Stuart Chappell invited you to join us at breakfast tomorrow, and I accepted for you."

"You *what?*" His shoulders sagged disconsolately. "Are you really going to make me go and be sociable to a bunch of golfers? It's horrible—I mean, good Lord, they're liable to start talking about *golf.*"

Lee, curiously enough, had never been able to get him interested in the game, which he persevered in thinking of as the most boring, pointless, and needlessly complicated waste of time ever invented. He followed her career with keen attention, but that was it. In the early days Lee had hoped to overcome this but he had resolutely resisted learning even the most elementary thing about it and she had long ago given it up as hopeless.

"Come on, buck up," she said, laughing. "It's only for an hour or so. And the point of it is that Stuart wants to talk to you privately afterward."

"About the kidnapping?"

She nodded. "He thinks he may know who's behind it."

He scowled at her. "So why tell me? It's the police he needs to talk to."

"That's what I told him. But he says he wants to talk to you first."

Graham shrugged, suddenly looking weary. "Well, it's up to him." He yawned hugely behind his hand. "I think jet lag's catching up to me. Let's sit down for a while and then head back."

They settled themselves at the back of the beach, where the dune grasses began, Graham with his back against a driftwood log, Lee against Graham, snug and cozy in the crook of his shoulder. He tipped his head to kiss her hair. The cedary scent of his aftershave mixed with the briny smell of the ocean. She wrapped her arms tightly around him, under his windbreaker, pressing her face against his chest.

"I love you. I think I'm even getting to like you without the mustache."

But he was already out. And two minutes later so was she.

*   *   *

They were jarred awake at 5:45 A.M. by the insistent, demented call of a whippoorwill from a tree across the road that was just behind them.

Lee stirred and groaned. She was cold and achy. There was dew on her jacket, her hair, her eyebrows.

"God," Graham said, unkinking himself from the log that by now was almost a part of him. "I think I know how Rip Van Winkle felt."

Lee squinted at the first muddy streaks of dawn lightening the sky over the mainland twelve miles away. "Were we really out here all night?"

"It sure feels like it," Graham said, getting his limbs working again. "I'm afraid your reputation is in tatters after all."

"Oh, I think I'll be able to sneak in before anybody's awake."

"I suppose so," he said, getting creakily to his feet and pulling her up too. "It's just too damn bad you have to go through the sneaking-in part without having had anything to sneak in about."

Lee laughed. "I know, it hardly seems fair."

"Well, there'll be other nights; we'll make up for it." They started walking back along the beach. "When do I show up for breakfast?"

"Eight-thirty, a quarter to nine. Enough time to shower and dress, thank goodness." She shook sand out of her hair. "I just hope there's some coffee out first."

"You'll sit near me, won't you? And Peg too? You won't just throw me to the golfers?"

"Come on, buck up," she said, laughing. "It's only for an hour or so, and then you can talk kidnapping with Stuart. You can do it."

"I'm not promising anything," he said dourly.

Chapter 10

But of course he charmed the socks off them, the females in particular, even before they were done milling groggily around the buffet table swilling down juice and coffee and making breakfast decisions. His fears of rampaging golf talk proved unfounded. Once they learned who he was they peppered him with kidnapping questions and opinions and hung on his every word. Darlene batted her eyelashes at him (not a pretty sight), and Ginny, although she didn't do anything flirty or provocative, couldn't help turning on like a lightbulb whenever he looked in her direction. For his part, Graham never seemed to notice those things, which greatly reassured Lee, who was in need of such comfort these days. How many Ginnys did he run into in his work? she wondered for the thousandth time. Bright, attractive, ambitious . . .

"No, I don't really agree with you," Graham was saying now, sounding more serious than he had so far. They had brought their food to the big table in the dining room, and were in a group that included Bert Balboni, Darlene, and—on either side of Graham as promised—Lee and Peg. Ginny, Frank, and Jackie were outside, eating on the terrace. Stuart hadn't appeared yet.

"I've been thinking about it," Graham continued, "and I have to tell you that in my opinion you're all taking it too lightly. I think she was in mortal danger."

"Little me?" Darlene actually said, or rather simpered—and, yes, batted her eyelashes again.

"Mortal danger?" Bert Balboni asked with a dismissive laugh. "As if." He even ate in a laid-back way, not using his fork so much to insert his food into his mouth as he did to wrist-flip it in. "The guy was helpless," he said, chewing. "I mean, here this huge bozo can't even handle a couple of pissed-off—"

"It was botched, all right," Graham said, "I'm not denying that. And I doubt if he'll be back, but if he'd succeeded in getting you into that truck yesterday, Darlene, I don't think anyone would have seen you alive again—whether your husband paid up or not."

That put an end to the sheep's eyes Darlene was making. "If you're trying to scare me," she said flatly, "you're succeeding."

Malcolm Labrecque, having taken more time than the others in weighing the array of options, and finally having decided on blueberry yogurt and a bran muffin, set his tray on the table, seated himself, and addressed Graham with scientific detachment.

"Are you saying they would have murdered her? That Lee saved her life?"

"Please!" Darlene said, and shoveled in some poached egg. It wasn't clear which of the two possibilities was more offensive to her.

Malcolm paid her no attention. He was, Lee had noticed earlier, not among those who deferred excessively to her. "But why would you assume that?" he asked Graham. He uncapped his container of yogurt and looked at it with unconcealed dissatisfaction. "Fruit on the bottom, dammit."

Because, Graham said, responding to the question, kidnappers, with their own future safety in mind, ordinarily went to great lengths to keep victims and bystanders from knowing what they looked like. Masks, hoods—

"And this guy just had a wig," Peg said. "There was nothing over his face. He didn't care whether she could identify him later or not, so that must mean . . ." She glanced at Darlene and let the rest of the sentence die away.

Not Malcolm. "That she would have been killed, yes."

Darlene eyed him balefully.

"That's right," Graham said quietly.

An abrupt pall descended on them. They looked uneasily at one another. Bert hummed something. A sullen Darlene drained her grapefruit juice.

"So!" said Peg. "What's the weather like in Paris this time of year?"

*　*　*

At 9:45 they heard Jackie's voice out on the terrace. "Wagons, ho-o!" he warbled in a phony Texas twang that sounded like a cross between Gabby Hayes and Woody Woodpecker. "Tahm t'maount up'n haid out oan th' rainge . . . the practice rainge, thet is."

Others finished their coffee, dabbed their lips, and otherwise prepared to leave. Stuart Chappell still had not made an appearance.

"Darlene?" Graham said. "I was supposed to talk to your husband this morning. Do you—"

"About what?" she asked bluntly.

"Well, I'm not sure, exactly. He—"

"Why would he want to talk to you?"

"I think," Lee said, "that he wanted to get Graham's thoughts on what happened yesterday."

That seemed to satisfy her, more or less. "Well, just don't tell him your theory about my getting murdered," she said to Graham. "He'd have a fit."

"Do you think he'll be down soon?" Graham asked.

"Don't ask me," she said, standing up. Then, realizing that that sounded a little peculiar, she added: "We're in different rooms. Stuart snores like a sea lion when he's not in his own bed at home, so I make him get another room. Go knock on his door if you want him. Two-eleven."

Ginny came over to the table as Darlene left. "You're looking for Stuart?" she asked Graham. "He's out on the beach. He's an early riser and so am I. We walk down there in the morning; it's peaceful and lovely in the fog. I left him there before breakfast. He's meditating on a rock."

Sounds like Stuart, Lee thought.

"He's what?" Graham asked.

"Sitting on a rock, meditating. It's a self-empowerment technique, or so he says. He's probably forgotten all about the time. Anyway, you can't miss him. First big rock on your right when you get there. There's a path down from in back. Gotta run, bye."

"Sitting on a rock, meditating," Graham mused, watching her leave. He smiled at Lee. "I suppose you gotta run too?"

"Actually, I don't. Jackie does his thing from ten to eleven. I'm not on for over an hour."

"Well, then, if I promise to get you there in time, how about walking on down to the beach with me? You can introduce me to Stuart. I may need help recognizing him. Probably a whole lot of people down there meditating on rocks."

✳   ✳   ✳

The mowed path began at a white, peeling gazebo on the back lawn of the inn, curved around a thick clump of black alder, ran down a dozen wooden steps, then changed to gravel and continued down the slope for a few hundred feet, cut through trailing brier and dense rushes along the shore of a salt pond, and finally took them over a plank footbridge onto the dunes of Ballard Beach. There was a thin morning overcast again, not enough to block the sun entirely but enough to mute everything with a cool, pastel cast.

It took Graham and Lee only five minutes to reach the beach, but when they arrived the first big rock on their right was occupied only by a couple of squabbling seagulls, and there was no sign of Stuart or anyone else on the shore.

"He must have come back while we were at breakfast," Lee said as they started back over the footbridge. "He's probably eating now, or up in his room."

"I guess," Graham muttered. "But for a guy who was so anxious to talk to me, you'd think—"

Lee stopped abruptly. "Oh, no," she said softly. Her hand rose to her mouth.

"What—" He followed the line of her gaze to the edge of the pond, alongside a boulder-blocked angle in the path. "Christ."

"It's Stuart," she said tonelessly.

It had to be Stuart. Who else wore brown-and-white wing tips? Who else wore argyles and plus fours? Beyond that she couldn't see, because only his feet and lower legs were clearly visible; the rest was under the surface of the reed-and-algae-choked water. He had been hidden from their sight by the boulder when they had come down a few minutes before.

Graham dropped quickly to his knees. Heedless of the sharp-spurred tangle of brier, he tugged on the argyle-covered ankles, hauling the body out of the water and onto the path. Lee watched, rooted to the spot, her heart lodged in her chest like a wedge of ice, as Graham bent to check for signs of life, then sat back on his heels with a sigh.

It was Stuart, all right. Trailing green algae, he was on his back, his arms above his head from having been dragged out of the water. His thinning gray hair, almost black from being wet, was plastered in sad, straggling wisps to his skull, and the neat little John Q. Citizen mustache had balled into ugly, dripping clumps, but it was still Stuart, and he was clearly beyond the help of CPR or any other earthly assistance. She tried to look away and couldn't. His face was weirdly lopsided, as if he were looking in two different directions at the same time. One pale, cloudy eye was mostly open, the other almost closed. His skin was an awful gray-blue . . .

"It's my fault . . ." she murmured in a dead voice. "He . . . he wanted to talk to you last night . . . I didn't tell you . . . I . . ."

"Lee," Graham said from his knees, "you'd better go on up to the inn and call Tolliver. I'll stay here."

She nodded. "Yes." But she didn't move.

He looked sharply at her. "Lee!"

She snapped out of her funk. "Yes, I'll go now." She turned and started up the hill.

But after two steps she heard his startled exclamation: "What the hell—" and she turned around.

Graham had pulled away some of the algae that had collected on Stuart's chest and he was staring at a thick, dull-metal rod projecting at an angle from the hollow of his throat.

He bent to look at it without touching it. "It's some kind of a, of a—I'm not sure what it is."

But Lee knew. She came a step closer to be sure, then turned, shaking, and ran up the hill to the telephone, her mind tumbling with shadows and crazy speculations.

Stuart Chappell had been murdered with the Paul Revere spike.

✳   ✳   ✳

"Did you want some more sherry?" Benny Trotter asked.

Lee shook her head, sipping from the wineglass without knowing it. She was still in a semi-daze. It's my fault, she kept thinking. He's dead because of my selfishness, because I couldn't bring myself to share Graham for a few hours. Someone murdered him to keep him from telling what he knew. If he had gotten to talk to Graham last night, there would have been no reason—

"Well, I sure would," Benny said, pushing himself heavily from his chair and lumbering to the area behind the bar. He poured himself a second brimming four-ounce glass, drank off half of it, topped it off, and returned to the table.

They were in the Keelboat Room, a small parlor off the lobby, with six or eight worn, overstuffed chairs and a few little tables with well-thumbed magazines on them, which served as a lounge for customers waiting to go in to lunch or dinner. Along one wall was a small, no-frills bar usually manned by Benny himself. The bar, like the restaurant, wouldn't open until noon, and Lee and Benny had the room to themselves. They hadn't turned on the lights, both preferring to sit in the relative dimness, illuminated only by gray, foggy light coming in through two windows in one wall.

He plopped himself back into the high-backed wooden rocking chair opposite her. "I just can't believe he's dead."

"No," Lee said.

They fell back into their own reveries.

From outside came the sound of a car pulling into the parking area. The door slammed, and footsteps crunched on gravel. Benny looked through a window to watch a figure hurry across the back lawn. Lee continued to stare at her glass.

"That's Dr. Heflin." He made it sound important.

"Dr. Heflin?" Lee asked dully.

"The police surgeon. Eye, ear, nose, and throat man, actually. But he knows his stuff," he assured Lee. "Not that he's ever had anything like this before. Tolliver either. Kind of surprising that your young fella is still out there with him. Been almost an hour now."

She almost smiled. Young fella. Graham would like that. He was thirty-two. Yesterday it was Stuart who had referred to him as her young man.

"Well, he used to be a policeman too; a detective," she said in the first try at conversation that she'd made since coming in from the path to call Tolliver. The sherry was finally reaching her, easing the sharp, stiff coldness in her chest, letting her think about somebody besides Stuart. "Or at least he was until a few months ago. Now he's a security consultant."

"That's nice," Benny said, not really listening. He finished his sherry and seemed to think briefly of going to the bar for another but changed his mind. "And you say . . ." he said, scratching at his beard and leaning forward.

She knew what was coming. Twice he'd asked and twice she'd told him, but he couldn't seem to get off the subject.

". . . that the spike was, that it was actually . . ."

"Benny, what *is* that spike?" The last thing she wanted to do was to describe the scene on the path one more time. "Why is it called the Paul Revere spike?"

He sat back, surprised. "Didn't I tell you?"

"No, you were going to but never did."

"Is that right? No, I guess I didn't, come to think of it. Well, let me get us some coffee."

"Let me do it," Lee said. She went to the pot on the heating pad at the back of the bar and poured two big cups, both black, both with sugar.

"Where do I start?" Benny mused. He held his cup in both hands, savoring it while he got the chair rocking slowly back and forth. He had turned dreamy and reflective. "What do you see when you look at me? Ho, ho, ho, a jolly old innkeeper, isn't that so? But I haven't been a jolly old innkeeper all my life . . ."

Chapter 11

Far from it. Benjamin Gabriel Trotter, now a comfortable, comforting old codger of seventy-one, had grown up in a well-intentioned but spartan orphanage in Baltimore. At twelve he ran away and joined the Depression-era army of hobos that was riding the rails from railroad yard to railroad yard across the United States. By the time he was sixteen he had been in jail twice, for vagrancy and for public drunkenness. An underage stint in the navy during World War II—he had been wounded twice, once by strafing from a Japanese fighter plane, once when his ship had been torpedoed—had straightened him out, but it hadn't settled him down. Restless and impetuous after the war, he spent the next twenty years wandering into and out of a dozen risky, precarious business ventures: a copper mine in Arizona, a fishing-boat charter service on the Gulf Coast, a mail-order poster and T-shirt business, a burrito factory in Houston.

In 1967, when he was forty-one and had actually managed to walk away with a few thousand dollars from the burrito factory, he got interested in marine salvage and teamed up with two like-minded younger men with similar dreams of Spanish galleons and New World treasure ships: Andy Gottlieb, a lawyer and an accomplished recreational diver; and a marine engineer named Stuart Chappell, then an ambitious twenty-eight-year-old.

"Hard to believe Stuart was ever twenty-eight, isn't it? Or that I was forty-one."

"Mm," Lee said.

Benny rocked back and forth, his eyes remote, lost in a distant past.

"The spike?" Lee prompted.

"I'm coming to it, I'm coming to it. I'm trying to give you the background." As did any good storyteller, he disliked having his rhythm thrown off.

"Sorry," said Lee. A wave of exhaustion flowed over her. She was suddenly washed out, limp. The horror on the path had finally begun to recede a little. She lay back in the overstuffed chair, more than happy to block it all out for a while and let Benny spin out his tale in his soft, singing tenor and in his own good time.

The three men, he told her, had bought an old lobster boat, rechristened it the *Virginia II,* and outfitted it with equipment mostly scrounged from surplus stores and marine junkyards. It hadn't taken them long to conclude that Spanish galleons were out of their league, and within a couple of years they had come to concentrate on the wreck-laden area around Block Island. Had Lee known that this was the graveyard of the North Atlantic Coast? That half of all the many wrecks in New England's treacherous waters had occurred off Block Island? That in 1881 seven schooners had broken up and gone down there in a single day?

"Hm? What? Uh, no, I didn't."

Well, they had, and Benny and his partners had even found a few of them, turning an occasional profit selling the relics at auction. But although they were able to keep themselves financially afloat, most of their anticipated "treasures" had turned out to be pipe dreams, and it was getting harder and harder to find backers. Benny, approaching forty-six, was starting to tire of it all. Now his dreams were more along the lines of settling down and running a bed-and-breakfast place on Block Island, which he had come to love.

Then, in 1971, in what was to have been their last venture, they hit it big at last. After months of research, calculation, and searching, they located the wreck of the bark *Good Hope*, which had broken up and gone down off the island in 1808, just off Black Rock Point, on its way from Providence to Canton with a load of—

"Spikes!" said Lee.

"Spikes?" Benny repeated, blinking. "No, not spikes. Flour, tobacco, beer, cutlery, and glassware. And luckily for us, a fair amount of the cutlery and glassware came through. Ah, you should have seen . . ." For a moment his eyes shone, but then the light went out of them. "I think I'll have just a teeny bit more sherry. Sure you don't want some? It's the good stuff."

Lee shook her head and watched him go back to the bar, pour half a glassful, and return to his chair, walking with exaggerated care, not drunk but not sober either. When he'd had a sip and continued, it was in a flatter, more subdued tone.

There had been a terrible tragedy on the very first day of serious diving. Andy had been killed in an accident; tangled in his own cables and hoses, he had been trapped on the ocean floor and drowned. That had done it for Benny; he wanted out of the business. The next day he sold his interest to Stuart for $15,000, enough for Benny to put a down payment on the Mooncussers Inn and set up as an innkeeper. Sure, Stuart was getting a bargain and they both knew it, but after all, Stuart was the one who would have to bear the expense of bringing the stuff up and of making it salable, and of trying to sell it at auction—which was always something of a gamble.

But in this case the gamble paid off handsomely; the wreck turned out to contain something even more valuable than its cargo—the four- to twelve-inch copper spikes that had held the hull together. Stamped with "US," they turned out to have been forged in the 1790s in Paul Revere's metal shop. Stuart retrieved over nine hundred of them, and he arranged with a Maine metalworking company to make decorative lamps and candleholders out of them, each one with a certificate of authenticity stating that the spike had been made by Paul Revere. The knickknacks sold for up to $200 apiece. Stu's profit on the lot was $120,000, Benny understood, and when added to what the cutlery (mainly bone handles, the metal having disintegrated) and glassware brought, he had walked away with over $200,000; to be exact, $208,000. In 1971 dollars.

"Wow," Lee said softly.

"Well, maybe 'walked away' isn't the right word," Benny said. "Stuart was never a man to shirk his obligations. He gave thirty thousand of it to Andy's wife and little girl. Oh, a very generous man was Stuart Chappell."

Her ears pricked. Had she heard a tinge of bitterness there? Resentment? Envy? The gears of her mind, stuck fast in self-recrimination and apathy until now, slowly began to turn again. Was Benny really the contented man he seemed to be? How had he felt about Stuart Chappell? Had he sat back complacently all these years, running his homey little ten-room inn, while Stuart built the money from their joint venture into an international, multimillion-dollar company? Or had he harbored some dark, deep-seated—

No, snap out of it, this was ridiculous. Benny Trotter was as nice an old coot as she'd ever run across. If she was already wondering if he might be a murderer, then there was something wrong with her, not him.

"Of course," he said, smiling a little with his eyes, "Stuart gave me something from the *Good Hope* too."

"Oh?"

He looked at her and slowly shook his head, as if in gentle wonder. "A spike," he said. "The Paul Revere spike. As a souvenir."

*   *   *

"What you need," Peg said in her best no-nonsense manner, "is some exercise. Let's rent a couple of bikes."

"What I need," said Lee, "is to sit right here."

"What, and sulk? And mope?"

Lee threw her a rare look of annoyance. "And think."

"Baloney, you don't have anything that needs thinking about." She had stood up only a second before, but now she sat down again in the white lawn chair beside Lee. "Lee, listen," she said earnestly. "You are not responsible for Stuart's death. How do you know it had anything to do with what he wanted to talk to Graham about?"

"Oh, come on, Peg, get real. His wife gets kidnapped—darn near, anyway—the day before yesterday, and today he's dead, murdered—the morning after practically telling me he knows who's behind it . . . and you want to tell me they're not related?"

"Yes, but even if they were, how were you supposed to know what was going to happen? It was a lousy break the way things turned out, that's all; a rotten, nasty break."

"A nasty break," Lee said with a short laugh. "That's one way to put it."

"Look, even if he'd had a chance to talk to Graham, who knows if Graham's advice would have been on target, if Stuart would have listened, if it would have kept him from getting killed even if he *did* listen . . . there are a million variables outside of your control. The only person responsible for Stuart's death is the person who killed him. Not you, not Stuart. The murderer. Period."

Lee sighed. "You're right, I know that. It's just . . ."

"It's just that you're upset, you're not seeing things clearly."

"And if you were in my place you wouldn't be upset? You'd be seeing things differently?"

Peg opened her mouth to say something, then clamped it shut. "That is completely beside the point. A diversionary tactic."

At that they both laughed. Lee hadn't realized how tight her jaw had gotten; it felt good to let her muscles relax a little. "Maybe a bike ride would be a good idea after all. But can we just go off without telling anyone?"

"So I'll tell someone," Peg said. "There's our trusty police chief. Be back in a sec."

They were on the back lawn of the inn, overlooking the Sound, right where Lee and Chief Tolliver had sat when he'd interviewed her after the kidnapping attempt two days before. The lawn had been a lively, galvanized place then, with most of the SRS crowd jabbering excitedly and maybe even a little happily about the attempt on Darlene. They were all there now too, having been summoned from the golf range, but there was no jabbering. Most of them stood not in laughing clusters but in a single quiet, edgy knot under the awning on the terrace, waiting to be questioned by Tolliver. At the far edge of the lawn Jackie dully and mechanically chipped three balls onto a level patch of grass about ten yards away, picked them up, and did it over again. And again. Darlene sat alone, as far as she could get from everyone else, having coldly, mutely rebuffed every offering of sympathy. She looked bleached and old; not grief-stricken, it seemed to Lee, but sullen and offended, as if angry that Stuart had had the nerve to get himself killed without checking with her first.

The portable bar had been rolled out, stocked with urns of coffee and hot water, as well as a basket of sweet rolls that would have gone untouched but for the two hungry young ambulance attendants in white jackets, who sat off by themselves, cheerfully munching. Stuart's body had yet to be carted off. It was still down there by the pond, out of sight. So were Graham, Dr. Heflin, Chief Tolliver, and a tall, wide-shouldered, crisply uniformed sergeant.

Lee had been the first person questioned by Tolliver, and he had asked her the same things he would shortly ask everyone else. When had she last seen Stuart? What had they talked about? Where had she been this morning before breakfast?

Where had she been last night?

That one made her hesitate, but she knew she could hardly hedge on something like this. She took a breath and told him that she'd spent the night on Crescent Beach.

The whole night? the chief wanted to know.

The whole night, she told him, praying that he wasn't going to ask the obvious next question, but of course he did.

"Anyone who can verify that?"

"Mr. Sheldon," she told him primly.

He looked up from his notebook.

"He was, er, with me," Lee said. "We were walking and we, we fell asleep, you see. We, ah . . . well, we fell asleep." How right Graham had been, she thought. If you were going to get yourself into embarrassing situations, the least you could do was to give yourself something worth being embarrassed about.

"Fell asleep," he said, still looking at her with a face about as noncommittal as a face can get.

"Yes." She was going to say more, then figured she was better off letting Graham handle it.

Tolliver didn't pursue it, thank goodness. He had more important questions: Did she know what Stuart wanted to talk to Graham about? Did he seem nervous, fearful? Could she remember his exact words? Did she know why he was reluctant to go to the police?

Lee told him everything she could; she had been over it in her own mind a dozen times. Stuart had wanted to talk to Graham about the kidnapping—the abduction, as he called it. He'd said something about knowing who was behind it. No, she didn't know why he wouldn't go directly to the police; he'd said something about it being embarrassing—no, awkward. And no, he didn't seem nervous or fearful. He seemed . . . well, he seemed like Stuart: vague, dreamy, abstracted, pleasant.

And dead, she thought miserably.

When Peg came back they walked into town, to the bicycle rental shop at the National Hotel. Lee got an all-purpose hybrid bike much like the three-speed that she kept stowed (and virtually unused) in a friend's garage in Portland; Peg was overjoyed to find a balloon-tired old Schwinn with upright handlebars and a buzzer built into the frame. They rode south on Spring Street, not speaking much, following it gently uphill (with Peg huffing) as it became Southeast Light Road and curved along the edge of the eroded sandstone cliffs that formed the island's southern border. At the top of a windswept rise they pulled up to give Peg a breather and to read a roadside granite marker.

Mohegan Bluffs
Elevation 183 ft.
In 1590 a war party of 40 Mohegan Indians
was driven over these bluffs by Block
Island Indians—the Manisseans.

In an obscure way it made Lee feel a little better. At least violent death wasn't anything new on Block Island. The marker had more to say:

Along this shore many vessels were wrecked.

Well, Lee knew something about that. She scanned the double column of ship's names: the *Lightburn*, the *Pocahontas*, the *John Davis*, the *Essex*, the *Meteor*, the *Jacob Winslow*. The final entry in the second column was a succinct, chilling *Etc.* Presumably that included the *Good Hope*, not important enough to make the list, but surely the only early-nineteenth-century ship ever to be involved—directly, physically involved—in a late-twentieth-century murder.

Peg's thoughts had been traveling along similar lines. "I've been thinking about Benny," she said a few minutes later as they stood on a weather-beaten viewing platform at the very edge of the bluffs, leaning on a wooden railing and overlooking a rocky beach far below and a restless, white-flecked Atlantic. Just behind them was the picturesque old Southeast Light, "the highest lighthouse in New England." The sun had broken through the fog but the breeze off the water was still cool. Lee had taken off the sun visor she'd been wearing and was letting the moist wind soothe her temples and stir her hair.

"About what you told me," Peg continued.

"And?"

"And whatever he felt or didn't feel about Stuart, I just can't see him being the one who—you know, did it."

"Me either," Lee agreed readily. "And not just because he's such a sweet old guy. He's not stupid. Why would he be crazy enough to kill anybody with something that's been lying on his own desk for almost thirty years? And do it right next to his own hotel, no less?"

"Right," Peg said. "And even if he did have it in for Stuart, why would he wait all this time to get even? Doesn't make any sense."

"Good," Lee said. "I'm really glad you feel that way. That lets Benny out of the investigation, then."

Peg let a few seconds pass and then turned to her with a faint, quizzical smile. "Are we doing an investigation?"

Lee had been more surprised than Peg to hear herself using the word. "Well . . . no, of course not. I only meant . . . well, you see, I guess I *do* feel a little responsible . . . I mean, not *really* responsible, but . . . I guess I don't know what I mean."

"*I* know what you mean. Somebody we both liked was murdered this morning. And whoever did it practically has to be one of the people we're here with; people we know." She started to tick them off on her fingers. "Bert, Malcolm, Ginny—"

"Now, wait a minute. You're jumping to conclusions. You can't just assume—"

Peg barked a laugh. "Now who needs to get real? Tell me, what's your hypothesis? That some outsider, some stranger, sneaked into the inn to kill Stuart early this morning without anybody's noticing, but then realized that he forgot to bring a weapon, so he picked up, of all possible things, the old Paul Revere spike that was on Benny's desk, then waited for Stuart to take his morning walk, then—"

"All right, all right. It had to be one of us. One of them. Probably."

"Definitely. Now, then, what I think we ought to do first—"

"—is go on back to the inn and have some lunch. I have this hollow feeling inside. I need something to eat."

"Okay, but after lunch I want us to find out—"

"Peg, has it occurred to you that Graham wouldn't be terrif-ically pleased to find out that we've been snooping around in po-lice matters? In a murder case? And that he just might have a point?"

Peg lifted her chin. "Snooping around? Me? My dear girl!" Then with a laugh: "That man sure has you cowed."

"Terrified," Lee said. "Let's head back."

Peg groaned and put a hand to her hip as she bent to pick up her bicycle. "Was this really my idea? It's the first time in cen-turies I've been on one of these things, and believe me, I'm feel-ing it. I hope I can make it. If I can't, just leave me by the side of the road. I'll get through somehow."

"You'll make it," Lee said, smiling. "It's downhill all the way."

"I just hope there's a tailwind," Peg said.

Chapter 12

The excitement was over by the time they got back to the inn. The ambulance and the police were gone, and there were two messages for them. One was a stiffly worded, photocopied memo from "Malcolm L. Labrecque, Executive Vice-President, Sea Recovery Systems" to "All SRS attendees and staff," with separate copies for Lee and Peg, telling them that they were expected at a two o'clock meeting in the Dory Room. "Please be prompt. There is much to discuss." Lee wouldn't have thought that she was "staff," but there was her name, *Ofsted, L.*, in the column at the bottom, neatly checked off.

The other message was more welcome. It was from Graham, telling them that he was having lunch at the place across from the ferry dock, the one with all the umbrellas out on the terrace, and why didn't they join him if they got back before one or so?

"The Harborside Inn," Peg said. "Great. We can drop the bikes off and walk there, assuming that my joints will still respond to my commands."

"You really ought to get some regular exercise," Lee said.

Peg drew herself up. "I play golf every weekend."

"Weekend golf," Lee said, "is hardly healthful exercise. Just look at the people you see out on the course, if you think it is."

They found Graham on the crowded, street-side terrace under one of the red-and-white umbrellas, spooning up clam chowder.

"Hi, how was the ride? What's wrong, Peg, something the matter with your foot?"

"With my foot, my ankle, my knee, my hip, you name it. It's called middle age."

"It's called being out of shape," Lee said as they sat down. "Peg is under the impression that sitting in a golf cart, getting out to swing a two-pound club once every ten minutes, and then getting back in the cart, is a form of exercise."

Graham smiled at her. She could read the relief in his eyes. She hadn't been in such wonderful shape herself when he'd last seen her. He leaned over to squeeze her upper arm.

"The chowder's terrific," he said, "and I've got a swordfish sandwich coming." He slid over a couple of menus. "I had the waitress leave these for you."

Peg took Graham's advice and ordered chowder and a swordfish sandwich. Lee, hollow feeling notwithstanding, couldn't quite face the idea of a hearty meal and ordered a simple salad of summer fruits.

While they waited, sipping iced tea, Graham filled them in on the events of the last few hours. In the first place, the police had asked everyone there to stay on for the next few days—

"Can they do that?" Lee asked.

"Can they *ask* them? Sure, it's just a request, not an order. Nobody's under arrest. And since you were all going to be here till Saturday anyway, it doesn't seem like too much of an imposition. Everybody's agreed to stay—well, everybody except Darlene; she wanted to go home to take care of family affairs and make funeral arrangements and so on, so of course they let her, but they know where to find her when they need her."

As for Stuart's body, it would be released to Darlene in a few days, but first it was on its way to Providence for an autopsy by the state medical examiner, not that there was much they expected to learn. They already had a good fix on the time of death—somewhere between 7 and 9 A.M., which fitted in with what Ginny had said about walking on the beach—and there wasn't much doubt about the cause of death—

"The spike," Lee murmured.

"No, I don't think so."

"You don't? But it was—it was . . ." She gestured at her own throat.

"Yes, but his skull was probably fractured first."

"I saw that there was something wrong with his head," Lee said, shutting her eyes briefly as the image of Stuart's misshapen face swam up in her mind, "but I assumed he hit it when he fell. On the boulder."

Graham shook his head. "No, I think the fracture came first. Then the spike. The police agree with me."

"How in the world can you tell something like that?" Peg asked.

"If you mean forensically, you can't. It's a question of logic. How do you walk up to somebody and plunge an eight-inch spike into his neck, and not too sharp a spike at that, without his making a pretty damn considerable fuss? You can't. But you *can* club him over the head from behind or beside him when he isn't expecting it—the site of the blow is the rear of the left parietal, by the way, just above and behind the ear—and then, when he's unconscious or even dead, you can drive the spike in without any trouble. You can use a rock to do it. If he's lying in a few inches of water you can do it without getting any blood on you."

Lee shuddered. Facing even a fruit salad wasn't going to be all that easy.

But Peg was entranced. "But *why*, Graham?"

"Obviously," he said, "to make a point."

Peg made a face. "If that's supposed to be a pun—"

He smiled. "No pun. The act of driving in that spike must *mean* something, at least in the killer's mind. Somebody told me it was from Benny's collection. I'm thinking about sitting down with him later, just casually, and seeing what he can tell me about it. He seems like someone who likes to talk."

"Oh, we can tell you all about the spike," Peg said.

There was a momentary pause. Graham put down his spoon. "Can you now?" he asked quietly.

Peg, for all her bluster, turned tail on the spot. "Well, *Lee* can. She was talking to Benny about it this morning."

Thanks a million, Peg; I owe you one, Lee thought as Graham's cool, blue, policeman's eyes swiveled in her direction.

He let out his patented world-weary sigh. "Now, look, Lee— look, both of you. We've been through this before, haven't we? I know you're only trying to help. I know you think you can use your charms to ferret out all this useful information that the police might otherwise never find out about. I know you mean well." He had started off in a low, reasonable voice—reasonable, that is, in the exasperating superior way that you'd reason with a four-year-old. But with every sentence his irritation grew. "But may I point out," he said between clenched teeth, "that this is *murder* we're talking about, that the policemen involved are highly professional and perfectly capable of handling the investigation themselves, and that you are not, repeat, not, a couple of cops, dammit!"

"Well, neither are you!" Lee shot back angrily, and then for good measure: "Dammit!"

"What the hell is that sup—" he began, then stopped dead in his tracks. "You're absolutely right. I'm not, am I?"

He looked so surprised that Lee couldn't help laughing.

Graham laughed too, a little sheepishly. "I'm sorry," he said. "I guess I was coming off there like, well, sort of like—"

"Sort of like an overbearing, supercilious jerk?" offered Peg, ever helpful.

"Sort of," Graham agreed. "But at least I do know what I'm doing when it comes to kidnapping and murder." He hesitated. "Besides, I'm involved with the case as a consultant."

"You mean the police have hired you?" Peg asked.

"Not exactly, no."

"So who's your client? Are you working for Darlene?"

"No, my client is Stuart. If you remember, Lee, you said he wanted my advice and was willing to pay for it. I agreed to meet with him, and as far as I'm concerned that makes him my client."

"Oh, yes?" Peg asked. "Tell me, in which world do you expect to get paid?"

"Not this one, I guess," Graham said wryly. "Look, all I'm trying to say is that I don't want you two taking foolish chances. It's not a game. There's a killer out there. If you happen to learn something that you think is useful, fine. Tell Tolliver right away. Or tell me, and I'll tell Tolliver. But no nosing around on your own, no hiding behind potted plants to eavesdrop on suspicious conversations, okay? Understood?"

Understood, they told him. "Scout's honor," Peg added soberly, bringing a scowl from Lee. With Graham, overkill was not the way to go.

"All right, then," he said doubtfully. "That's that." Then he surprised them by laughing. "I should tell you, the speech I just gave you was just about word for word what Chief Tolliver told *me*. When the body got shipped off they gave me my walking papers. They appreciated my help, they're highly aware of my expertise, they're grateful for my willingness to assist—but they'd just as soon handle it themselves, thank you."

"But that's ridiculous!" Lee said. "You were a police lieutenant yourself until a few months ago. And now you're an international—"

Graham shook his head. "No, it's the right thing for them to do. I'm a private citizen. I have no more business than you do getting underfoot in an official investigation. If I were in charge here, I'd have said the same thing."

"But—"

"Now," he said, "what's this about the spike?"

While they ate their meals Lee told him about the history of the Paul Revere spike, about the *Good Hope*, about everything Benny had told her. Graham paid strict attention.

"This other diver, the one who was killed—"

"Andy Gottlieb," Lee said.

"Andy Gottlieb. Was there any kind of investigation into his death?"

"If there was, Benny didn't say so. But it was an accident, why would there be an investigation?"

Graham thoughtfully studied the underside of the umbrella. "Tangled up in his cables on the ocean floor. Lots of room for different interpretations there. I don't know about Block Island, but most jurisdictions automatically investigate any accidental death under ambiguous circumstances. Maybe there's a record of it."

"You think there's a connection?"

He continued to study the spokes on the underside of the umbrella. "To Gottlieb's death, I don't know. To the *Good Hope*,

I'd say yes, or at least it's a good place to start. That spike has to mean something."

"Graham," Peg said abruptly, "what was the exact amount in that ransom note, do you happen to know? Six hundred thousand and what?"

"Yes, I asked Tolliver," he said, reaching behind him for a notepad in the pocket of the windbreaker that was draped over the back of his chair. He flipped pages. "It was . . ." He looked up at Peg. "Why, what's the difference?"

"Come on now, I want to know. Don't worry, no lurking behind potted plants, I promise. I just want to run a few ideas through my laptop."

"Six hundred and fifty thousand, nine hundred and ninety-three dollars," Graham said.

"No cents?"

"Not that I recall. Just a nice, round six hundred and fifty thousand, nine hundred and ninety-three."

"Is that kind of thing common in kidnappings?" Lee asked.

"Common, no, but once in a while you do get an oddball number. Some wacko who's into numerology, or someone who fancies he's owed some specific amount of restitution, or compensation, or debt, or something. One thing it tells me is that we're not dealing with any kind of terrorist group or professional kidnapping ring. This is amateur stuff."

"But we knew that anyway, didn't we?" Lee said. "It just about has to be somebody here at the SRS meeting. Doesn't it?" she added when he didn't respond.

"It looks that way. Which is all the more reason for none of us to go blundering around mucking up things for Tolliver." He looked at his watch. "It's one-forty-five. You two have your session with Mr. Labrecque coming up in fifteen minutes. We probably ought to start strolling up the hill."

He ran his eyes over the check and reached for his wallet. "I'll pick up the tab," he said.

Peg reached for her bag. "No, I'll pick up the tab."

"Boy, I'm sure glad I know all these rich people," Lee said.

*   *   *

Of the public rooms at the Mooncussers Inn, the Dory Room was the plainest, the most purely functional. No busy Victorian wallpaper, no gauzy curtains, no lushly padded chairs with curved arms of dark, polished wood, no ornate lamps hanging from the ceiling. And despite its name, no nautical embellishments. Just a no-frills conference room with an acoustic-tile ceiling, lit by a bank of neon lights and furnished with stackable plastic chairs surrounding a pressed-board, wood-grained, Formica-topped conference table taking up the center of the room.

Down one side of the table were Peg, Lee, and Frank Wishniak. Opposite them were Ginny Briggs and Jackie Piper. The chair next to Ginny was vacant. At the head, looking very much at one with the workaday setting, was Malcolm Labrecque. He had changed from his golf clothes to a snuff-colored suit and a tie, but his jacket was draped over the back of his chair and the cuffs of his white shirt folded manfully over his scrawny forearms. In front of him was a meticulously arranged sheaf of printed material. For a good five minutes now, he had been steadily pressing and releasing the push button on his ballpoint pen, *ge-click, ge-cluck, ge-click, ge-cluck,* either oblivious to or unconcerned with the upward-rolling eyeballs, grinding teeth, and meaning-laden glances that increased in number and emphasis with each *ge-cluck.*

"Now I know what Chinese water torture is like," Frank grumbled to Lee.

The leisurely entrance of Bert Balboni on his cloud of aftershave and breath freshener brought the clicking to a merciful end. A soft sigh of relief rose from the group.

"According to my watch," Malcolm said pointedly, "it's now eleven minutes after two."

Bert glanced at his own wrist. "Nope, you're off by a minute, Mal. It's two-ten."

"This meeting was scheduled for two o'clock."

Bert sauntered to the one free chair beside Ginny, eased his heavy body comfortably into it, and took his time before replying. "Since when does an SRS meeting scheduled for two start at two? I figure I'm five minutes early."

A ligament at the back of Malcolm's jaw, just in front of his ear, made an audible snapping noise. "Since I took charge."

"Oh, hey, wow, are you in charge? I guess I didn't realize you were running the whole company." His speech was just a little overcareful, just a little slurred. He'd been drinking, or maybe he was always a little drunk. He touched his hand to his forehead and breast. His gold-link chain necklaces clinked. "Felicitations, esteemed leader. You have but to speak, and I obey."

Ginny threw him a black look. "Grow up, will you?" The words, uttered in a disgusted whisper, emerged by chance into a moment of otherwise perfect silence and could be clearly heard around the table.

Bert flushed darkly and turned on Ginny. "You wanna talk about being grown-up? You wanna talk about mature, responsible behavior? You—"

"Knock it off, Bert," Frank said. "This isn't the place."

Bert glared at him, then shrugged. "Screw you. Hey, esteemed leader, where's the coffee? Don't tell me you forgot to get us any coffee."

"Yikes," Peg said under her breath. "I hope I remembered to bring my conflict-resolution pills." Lee felt for her. If Peg's job was to mend hard feelings and "develop an atmosphere of team-work and cooperation," she was going to be earning her fee and then some.

While Malcolm fumed, searching for a comeback, Frank Wishniak took up the slack. "Malcolm, we're all here now," he said reasonably. "Why don't we get started?"

"Very well," Malcolm said, "now that everyone has managed to find their way here at last. To begin with, it seems to me that as long as we are going to be here in any case, we may as well continue with the primary purpose of this retreat. This morn-ing's events were extremely regrettable, but there's no point in our throwing away time and money on top of them."

"That's the trouble with Malcolm," Frank said to Lee from the side of his mouth. "The man's nothing but a mushy, pulsat-ing blob of sentiment."

"Therefore," Malcolm continued, patting the pile of paper, "I've used the last few hours to prepare handouts proposing the implementation of new strategic subsystem parameters for—"

"*Malcolm, for God's sake!*" Ginny exclaimed, so abruptly that Jackie, sitting next to her, practically bolted out of his chair. "Stuart has only been dead a few hours! He's not even . . . how can you possibly—" Red-eyed, breathless, her emotions as tightly coiled as her copper-wire hair, she seemed on the verge of losing control and flying into pieces but pulled herself to-gether with a visible effort, lowering her voice and speaking with her eyes closed, forcing out one slow, resistant word at a time. "I think, out of respect for Stuart, we should give over the rest of the day to his memory. If you want, we can work tomorrow." She opened her eyes and fixed them on Malcolm. Not . . . today."

"Ginny, you don't seem to realize—"

"I'd have to agree," Peg cut in. "This wouldn't be a good day to make any important decisions."

"Second," said Frank.

"Third," Bert said.

Faced with his first insurrection, Malcolm glanced at Lee as if for support, but Lee lowered her eyes, hardly able to look at him. What kind of cold, bloodless fish of a man—

"All right," said Malcolm, apparently deciding on a temporary retreat, "you may be right. We'll wait until tomorrow morning. Eight o'clock."

"Eight o'clock!" cried a stricken Bert.

"Eight o'clock," Malcolm repeated, passing out the handouts. "Please study these tonight. I will want your comments. Peg, you'll be prepared to facilitate?"

Peg nodded. "If you like."

"All right, then, I'll see you all—"

"What about the golf, Malcolm?" Jackie asked.

"Yes? What about it?"

"Do you want us to continue with the program?"

"Under the circumstances, I don't really . . ." He paused. "I assume there would be a *pro rata* refund for the unfinished part of the course?"

"I'm afraid not. I've had to commit the entire week. My bookings are made months ahead, and there's no way I can recoup at this point."

"I understand that, but you can hardly expect—"

"It's in the contract, Malcolm," Jackie said with a steely new edge to his voice. "If you want to cancel the rest of it, that's your affair. But you pay for the full program."

Malcolm pondered, debating with himself. "Well, perhaps we might enjoy it at that," he said with a halfhearted try at good fellowship. "But I doubt if we're going to be able to spare more than a few hours a day. There's much work to be done."

Jackie gave him an agreeable nod. "Whatever."

"Then that's all there is to say for today," Malcolm said. "Thank you for your attention." He began gathering up the notes that he'd brought. "Peg, if you wouldn't mind staying to confer?"

Bert was the first one out of his chair. "Bar's open," he grunted, heading in that direction.

And leaving on the table, untouched, his copy of "Proposed New Strategic Subsystem Parameters."

Chapter 13

"What are you drinking?" Bert asked from behind the un-manned bar in the Keelboat Room, where he was helping him-self to the Cutty Sark bottle. Like Malcolm, he had changed out of the morning's golf clothes but had chosen a different sartor-ial direction: soft camel-hair blazer, robin's-egg-blue trousers, al-ligator loafers, open-throated shirt, two or three neck chains with things dangling from them—a cross, a shark's tooth, other unidentifiable objects hidden in the puff of pale hair on his chest. In short, Mr. Hollywood.

"Club soda would be nice," said Lee.

"Living dangerously, huh?" Bert scooped ice into two glasses, got a plastic tub of lime wedges from the refrigera-tor—obviously he knew his way around behind the Moon-cussers' bar—put the wedge in one glass and two inches of Scotch into the other, filled them both with soda, and handed Lee's to her.

"Cheers."

"Cheers," said Lee. She had gone to the Keelboat Room pri-marily because she wanted a soft drink, but also because she thought that was where most of the others might drift to. But the others had gone elsewhere, and she and Bert had it to them-selves.

Bert downed a third of his drink, refilled the glass from the Scotch bottle, and addressed the wall. "Can you believe that guy?"

"Malcolm?" Lee said.

"Malcolm, of course Malcolm. I never thought I'd say it, but maybe working for Stu wasn't so bad. At least his head was on right. But Malcolm . . ." More Scotch and soda went down. "What a turd."

"Well, he probably feels that he's responsible for SRS now, and that it's important to, um, you know—"

"Yeah, 'um, you know' is right. Look, the reason Malcolm is in such a rush is because he can't wait to run things without Dar-lene around to butt in, for a change."

"But he's the executive vice-president, isn't he? Darlene can't overrule him, can she?" A thought occurred to her. "Or does *she* own the company now? Did Stuart leave it to her?"

"I'm supposed to know that? I'll let you in on a secret: Stu didn't exactly confide in me." He was crouched down, rummag-ing in an under-the-bar pantry now, finally coming up with a bag of cheese-flavored corn chips. "Or anybody. But if it comes down to a contest between the Grand Czarina and the Human Adding Machine, my money's on Darlene."

He ripped the bag open with his teeth. "Oh, Christ, here come the yes-people. Let's get some fresh air." He plopped the bag into her hands. "I'll bring the drinks." He turned and started toward the lobby and the front door without a backward glance as Ginny and Frank, heads down, deep in conversation, approached from the other direction. Lee went after Bert with-out a second's hesitation. Never mind that Balboni was generally unappetizing. He was in a talkative mood, he was on the outs with his colleagues, and he was, if not quite drunk, then well on the way. Who knew what might come out of a combination like that?

He was in a corner of the front porch, sitting in a rocking chair, rocking away with one ankle crossed over the other knee and looking out over the now-familiar island scenery: farmhouses, rolling hills, stone fences. Lee put the bag of corn chips on a wicker table next to him, pulled up a nearby deck chair, and waited for him to get things off his chest.

And waited. Bert methodically popped chips into his mouth, keeping time to the rocking of the chair.

Well, then, it was up to her. Fishing time. "Awful about Stuart," she said, sipping her club soda.

"Yeah, poor guy," he said absently.

"Who could possibly have done a thing like that?" She made it sound as much like an idle question as she could. Graham's objections aside, she didn't want to get the reputation of being too inquisitive about Stuart's death. One of the very small, very tight (if not overly compatible) group of people at the Mooncussers was almost certainly a killer and would hardly take kindly to her nosing around. Maybe it was the very man she was talking to, although it was hard for her to believe. On the other hand, it was hard to believe it about any of them. Ginny? Frank? Malcolm?

"What gets me," Bert said, methodically rocking and chomping away, "is what a cheapshit, penny-ante, dried-up little crud he is. I mean, the guy hates golf, right? He thinks it's a complete waste of time, right? That we have a lot more important things to do. Right?"

It took her a confused second to realize he was still going on about Malcolm. "I guess that's true, yes."

"But the idea of paying for something he doesn't get drives him up the wall. So now we keep on with the golf lessons even though they're completely, you know, counterproductive as far as he's concerned. Is there a loose screw there, or what?" He drank from the glass in his hand, recoiled, and stared accusingly at the glass. "What *is* this stuff?"

"I think you have my drink," Lee said.

"Uch."

He handed it to her. Lee put it on the table, no longer thirsty. Bert picked up his Scotch and took a slug, swirling it around his mouth to get rid of the offending taste of club soda and lime. "Not that what he does with SRS's money is any of my business. No, they're not going to have old Bert to kick around much longer."

"You're leaving?"

He hunched his shoulders and looked sly. "We'll see. Got a few other irons in the fire. And the last thing Marvelous Malcolm wants is me hanging around. I cramp his style, haven't you noticed? Darlene's not too keen on having Benny's favorite nephew around either."

She frowned at him. "Benny's nephew? You're Benny's *nephew*?" But why had Benny failed to mention it to her? It seemed like an odd thing not to have gotten around to at some point.

"Sure, you didn't know that?" He stared at her, definitely a little tiddly now. "No, how would you know a thing like that. Yeah, he's my Uncle Benny, there's no secret about it. That's how come I got hired. Stu never made any secret out of it. It was atonement, blood money, whatever you want to call it. Ah, what the hell."

"Blood money?" she echoed to keep him going.

It took him a second to answer. "That's right. Benny and Stu used to be in business together. I bet you didn't know that either." He gave her a bleary smile.

"They *did*?" The stunned amazement in her own voice

brought a wince. Let's not overdo it here, kiddo. High drama was hardly called for, and Lee had never been a very good actress. She just wanted to keep him talking, to hear his viewpoint on Benny and Stuart and the old days. Fortunately Bert was too soused to recognize baloney when he heard it.

"Yup," he said, "it's a long story."

It was; rambling and maudlin and self-serving, but essentially the same story that Benny had told her that morning. How Benny and Stuart and Andy Gottlieb had hunted sea treasure years before. How they'd found the *Good Hope*. How Gottlieb had been killed in an underwater accident. (No, Bert didn't know the details. A kinked air hose or something.) How Stuart had bought out Benny. And how Benny had used the money to buy the Mooncussers Inn and Stuart had used his profits to launch SRS.

"But what does that have to do with your working there?" Lee asked. "What did you mean, 'blood money'?"

"I *told* you," Bert said. (He hadn't.) He rearranged himself in the rocking chair and put his feet up on the railing. "One day, Stu comes up to Benny and says: 'Hey, old pal, since I screwed you over royally when I cheated the hell out of you on the *Good Hope* so that now I'm running a multimillion-dollar international company while you're running this cheesy hotel in the middle of nowhere, what do you say I make it all up to you by giving a job to your deadbeat nephew?'"

"Oh, I'm sure he wouldn't have—"

"So Benny, being Benny, falls all over himself with gratitude and tells me what a great deal it is and I should take it. And I did, why not? The pay was good, the work wasn't bad, and my last two jobs were disasters, what with the cretins I had for bosses." A slow, rueful grin spread across his face. "And what do you know, contrary to all predictions the deadbeat nephew actually worked out. I'm the guy that put SRS on the map, not that Stu ever bothered to thank me. My contacts, my connections, my being in the right place at the right time. I quadrupled Stu's client list. Me."

He drained his Scotch and soda and balanced the emptied glass on his stomach. "And what do I get for it?" he asked himself. "When it's time to pick a veep, who gets the nod? Malcolm, can you believe it? *Malcolm!*"

He snorted his contempt and lifted the glass to his mouth again but got only ice cubes. He looked irritably around; at the table, at the floor. "Didn't you bring the bottle out?"

"I'll get you another drink," Lee said.

"Atta girl."

In the bar she briefly considered pouring straight Scotch to keep him going but decided there really wasn't any need to lubricate him any more than he already was. Any drunker and he'd be asleep. She put in half a jigger of whiskey, filled the glass with soda, and added a couple of drops of Scotch to the top to make it smell stronger.

He wasn't asleep when she got back to the porch, but he was getting close, sitting just as she'd left him, with his eyelids starting to drift down and a goofy, loose-lipped smile on his face.

He took the drink and went on speaking, slowly, mournfully, as if there had been no interruption. "Still, I never expected to be here fifteen years later, but life's like that, you know? Looking back, you can see how it all sort of makes sense, but if someone told you back then how it was going to work out you'd laugh at him. That's my philosophy."

Philosophizing made Bert sleepier yet. He settled deeper into his chair and propped his feet farther up on the rail. Frank and Ginny came out onto the porch, saw them, and turned around and headed for the far corner. Bert, three-quarters asleep, watched them go.

"Now, there's the little lady I feel sorry for," he said.

"Ginny? Why?"

"No more Big Daddy to protect her; she's on her own now."

"Stuart was protecting her?"

Bert chuckled thickly. "He was doing a lot more than protecting her." He opened a drowsy eye to peer at her. "You're telling me you didn't know they had a thing going?"

"Stuart and *Ginny?*" This time the amazement was genuine.

"Christ, that's common knowledge. Didn't you ever *see* them together? Everybody knew about it. Ask Frank. Ask M—"

"Including Darlene?"

"Sure, she'd have to be . . ." He yawned copiously. "She'd have to be blind not to know. She'd . . ."

That was it, he was sound asleep and snoring. Lee took the glass from his hand, put it on the table, and quietly left.

☆ ☆ ☆

Her dinner with Graham was a subdued affair. With his having to catch a 5:45 charter to Boston in order to make a Delta flight that would get him to Toronto that night, they had an early meal of hamburgers at the Airport Restaurant, a down-home kind of place in the little terminal, with a counter, a few tables, and old wooden propellers hanging on the walls. Peg, claiming a prior appointment with her laptop, had declined to come; Lee was fairly sure that she had simply wanted to let them say goodbye on their own.

"We just said hello," Lee said, "and now we're saying goodbye."

"I'll be back in a couple of days."

They picked at their burgers and French fries. Lee told Graham what she'd learned from Bert, and Graham told Lee what he'd heard from Benny: that Andy Gottlieb's death had come about when his lines had gotten fouled while he was on the ocean floor burrowing into the *Good Hope*. The ship was about to be driven onto the rocks at Black Rock Point, and Benny and Stuart had been forced to cut Andy's lines.

Lee put down her hamburger. "*Cut!* You mean they had to . . . kill him?"

"I don't know that I'd say quite that."

"They were responsible for his death, then."

"I don't know that I'd put it that way either."

"Well, how would you put it?"

"The way Benny remembers it, Andy would have been killed if they *didn't* cut him loose because he was caught in a narrow passage in what was left of the *Good Hope* and the violent movement of the boat on the surface would have dragged him into the timbers. This way at least he had a chance to get up to the surface himself. That's the way he remembers it, anyway."

"But you don't believe him?"

He tipped his head to one side. "I don't have any reason not to believe him but . . . well, it's something he's not very comfortable with. I had to drag it out of him."

"I wouldn't be very comfortable with it either. However you put it, they cut his air hose. And he died."

Graham nodded. "Apparently it was Stuart who actually did the cutting."

"That's easy for him to say, Graham, now that Stuart isn't here to speak for himself. It's not that I think Benny's necessarily lying, but it was a long time ago. Memories get fuzzy, especially ones you'd prefer not to remember."

"No, I've been to the police department, I've seen the case file on the accident, and that's the way both of them told it at the time too. Benny never faulted Stuart. He thought it was the right thing to do too, he was just too unglued to do it himself. So Stuart had to. Andy's body was recovered from the *Good Hope* by police divers the next morning. Cause of death: aspiration of fluid into the air passages. Drowning." He gave up on his hamburger and pushed the plate away. "What are you thinking?"

"I'm thinking," Lee said slowly, "how this is starting to get strange. In 1971 Stuart cut the air hose on a young diver who was down working in the *Good Hope.* The diver died, but Stuart got rich selling spikes from the wreck. Then, over a quarter of a century later, Stuart himself is found dead—with one of those very same spikes through his throat." She looked at him, eyebrows lifted.

"That's an awfully long time to wait for revenge," Graham said.

"I'm not saying it's revenge, I'm saying—gosh, I don't know what I'm saying." She shook her head, rubbed her eyes. "What a day. Did you tell Chief Tolliver about this?"

"Sure. We looked at the file together." He reached across the table to smooth her hair. "Let him worry about it, Lee. You look absolutely bushed."

She pressed his hand against the side of her head and smiled. "I didn't get a very good night's rest last night. Somehow, I seem to have spent the whole night out on the beach. Did the chief ask you about that, by the way? I had to tell him."

"Oho," Graham said, laughing, "so *that's* what he meant."

"By what?"

"Never mind." He looked out the window at the runway, where a lone, twin-engine plane taxied slowly toward them, engines clattering. "There's my ride. Damn, I hate to leave you."

She stood up with him. "You'll be back Saturday morning?"

"Right, as early as I can." He swung his duffel bag onto one shoulder. "I'll call you tomorrow from Toronto. Finish your hamburger. Put all this out of your mind." He kissed her on the forehead. "And get some sleep."

She followed his advice to the letter, taking what was left of her meal back to the inn and finishing it in her room while mindlessly watching a *Mannix* rerun. Both the reception and the group dinner had been called off, and by nine o'clock she was under the covers and asleep, her windows thrown open to the breeze and to the hollow, melancholy calls of nightjars, owls, and other winged hunters of the night.

*   *   *

In 1957 the legendary golfer Ben Hogan published what would become one of the all-time classics of golf instruction: *The Modern Fundamentals of Golf.* It was far too mechanical for Lee's taste (even the "waggle," the preliminary little jiggle of the club most golfers make before beginning their swings, had four full pages and five detailed illustrations devoted to showing you precisely how it was to be done), but the clarity of its instruction had never been equaled.

Among its contributions was Hogan's concept of imagining the plane of the backswing as a large, inclined pane of glass with a hole in it near one end. This imaginary pane would rest on the golfer's shoulders (with his or her head through the hole), while the far end would rest directly on the ground a few inches on the other side of the ball. The idea was to take the club back parallel to and under this angled pane of glass, taking particular care never to raise the clubhead above the plane and thus "shatter" the glass at any point in the swing.

Since then the imaginary pane of glass had been a mainstay among teaching professionals. In forty years no one had come up with a way of improving on it.

Until Jackie Piper came along. Jackie did what none who came before had done or thought of: he reasoned that if an imaginary pane of glass was such hot stuff, a real one would be a knockout. The result was the newest Piper product: the Personal Plane Partner. This was an inclined, nine-by-seven-foot pane of glass (actually Plexiglas) with a head-sized hole near the upper end and four adjustable, splayed, rubber-tipped metal legs, that anyone could take home for his very own for $89.95 ($76.46 with the 15 percent discount). Jackie had brought four of the new devices to Block Island.

So it was that on Thursday morning at 10:05 a bemused Lee stood near the Quonochaugachaug practice range watching an astonishing sight: four grown, otherwise sane-looking people standing in a close-set row—Ginny, Bert, Peg, and Frank—each of them with his or her head sticking up through a hole in a transparent, rectangular panel, each of them taking half-swings in slow motion at an invisible ball, while an animated Jackie bounced up and down in front of them giving instructions and encouragement.

It was like a scene out of *Planet of the Apes*, where some gesticulating chimp frolicked and gibbered in front of a sorry line of shackled, broken humans. Only these humans seemed to be having a good time.

"Don't laugh," Peg called to her. "This could be you."

Not on your life, Lee thought, slipping her putter from her bag and getting a bucket of balls. There was about an hour before she was due to give putting instruction and she could stand a little practice; putting was not her long suit. Besides, it would be lovely to focus for a while on something that wasn't murky and sordid, something satisfyingly clean and simple, like stroking a little white ball into a little black hole, all on a field of perfect, green grass.

She had tried two twenty-footers, coming reasonably close on both, when she looked up to see Ginny at the edge of the green. "Hi, through already?"

Ginny shook her head. "I just couldn't concentrate. I'm . . . it's a little hard to get into the mood."

Lee nodded sympathetically. Ginny, so strong and capable yesterday and the day before, looked like hell this morning, as if she'd been up crying all night. Hollow, pink-rimmed eyes, gray complexion, sunken mouth, no makeup. For the first time she looked her thirty-five years and then some. Only her hair was as energetic as usual, which made the rest of her all the more drab by comparison. And she was worrying her lower lip with her teeth so fiercely that any second Lee expected to see blood. Stuart's death had hit her hard, that was clear—harder than it had hit Darlene, who had reacted with a stolid, cold self-composure. Ginny looked on the verge of breaking down and bawling, in fact, and very much in need of someone's shoulder to do it on.

Lee felt for her but held back. She was far from hard-hearted, but she couldn't help recoiling from emotional displays. And Ginny looked as if all it would take to set her off was a kind word. Besides, did one offer condolences to a deceased married man's mistress? Wife, yes, but girlfriend? She didn't think so. And besides that, as far as Ginny was concerned, Lee didn't know anything about Ginny's relationship with Stuart.

"I could stand a cup of coffee," Lee said, the best she could come up with under the circumstances. "Want to go over to the shed with me and have some?"

Ginny smiled shakily. "All right." The tears welled up. Her eyes shone.

Oh, God, Lee thought, here it comes. She looked desperately toward the row of golfers. Where was Peg when you needed her? Good old, sensible, warmhearted, bluff-talking Peg. But, no, her friend still had her head stuck through that ridiculous sheet of plastic, totally absorbed in trying to follow Jackie's instructions.

To Lee's relief, however, Ginny coughed once or twice and managed to fight the emotion down. "You know what would really be nice?" she asked. "To get away from the course for a little while, maybe take a drive." She lowered her eyes. "Would you like to come?"

"I have to teach at eleven."

"We'd be back by then. I just want to look at the coast for a few minutes." She laid a tentative hand on Lee's forearm. "Please. I could use some company."

"Okay," said Lee after a moment's hesitation. "How much difference can another forty-five minutes make to my putting?"

They took one of the rental cars that the group had used to get out of the course and drove out onto Cooneymus Road with Lee at the wheel.

Chapter 14

There was general agreement afterward that Frank Wishniak's cigar had started the inexorable chain of events that led to the spectacular end of the day's instruction with the Personal Plane Partner.

Frank, who had been doing unexpectedly well with the device (in slow motion his swing was a thing of beauty, something like the underwater glide of a graceful hippo), had been encouraged by Jackie to see what might happen if he tried a full-speed, full-length backswing. Frank happily complied, but with his bulbous torso pretzeled into the unique Wishniak take-away his clubhead banged into the Plexiglas, jarring him to the extent that the ever-present dead cigar fell from his mouth, whereupon his right hand instinctively jerked up to catch it. But with the nine-by-seven-foot plastic pane sitting on his shoulders this was impossible. His hand struck the pane, tilting it to the left. His body, already wildly off balance, tilted it further. The unfortunate result was that the two metal legs on the left side of the Personal Plane Partner—the short one in front, the long one in back—gave way at their hinges, and the plastic, with Frank's three chins still wedged in the hole, toppled sideways, taking Frank with it.

The *really* unfortunate part was that the three Personal Plane Partners had been set up side by side—Frank's, Peg's, and Bert's—so that the three golfers were standing shoulder-to-shoulder, or rather Plexiglas-to-Plexiglas. When Frank went, they all went. Metal legs collapsed, clubs flew, arms and legs flailed. Even the empty one that Ginny had been using toppled. They all wound up in a clattering heap, Bert on his back with his legs waving in the air like an upended beetle, Frank on his side, sputtering and still wedged into his Plane Partner, Peg on her rump, more or less caught between them—all of them miraculously unhurt and laughing like crazy.

Jackie watched, amazed into silence for the whole ten seconds or so that it took for the sequence to unfold. When the racket died away at last, he said reflectively: "You know, it could be there are still a few bugs in this thing that need ironing out," bringing on fresh gales of laughter.

"You ought to issue a product recall," Frank said, getting his head out of the hole with Peg's help. "This thing's life-threatening."

"Hey, Frank," Bert said, "why don't you sue him? Maybe if you won you could afford to light one of those cigars sometime."

"*Not* funny!" cried Jackie. "Joking about product liability suits is callous and insensitive, didn't you know that?" He cast a mournful eye over the wreckage of his Personal Plane Partners. "Why don't you all take a break? I'll see if any of this is redeemable."

"Sorry about that," said Frank as he headed toward the shed with Peg and Bert. "That damn thing gave me claustrophobia to begin with. Reminded me of those fifty-pound diving helmets we used in the old days."

"Did you used to be a diver, then?" Peg asked.

"Did he used to be a diver!" Bert said, laughing. "Who do you think taught Stuart everything he knew?"

"Really, is that true?" asked Peg.

Frank looked pleased. "Well, I wouldn't go as far as all that, but I guess I showed him a few things about salvage diving that he didn't know before. Stuart and I go back to 1971, did you know that?"

"No, I didn't."

"Yep. For the first seven years of SRS, it was just me and him. We started the outfit together."

"That's fascinating," Peg said. Nineteen seventy-one, she was thinking. The year of the *Good Hope's* salvage. Had Frank been part of that? Had he helped bring up the spikes that had made Stuart's fortune—but not his own? How had he, the firm's senior employee, felt when Stuart picked the much younger Malcolm for the vice-presidency? There were all kinds of intriguing angles here . . .

"I'd love to hear about it over a cup of coffee," she said.

"It makes a pretty interesting story," Frank agreed. "Come on, I'll fill you in. Hey, you think there are some of those jelly donuts left?"

*   *   *

"Turn right," Ginny said when they got to Center Road. "That's Fresh Pond over there." And a minute later: "And that's Peckham Pond. And Dahl's Pond is up ahead on the right. They say there are three hundred and sixty-five ponds on the island, one for every day of the year."

"I can believe it. You seem to know Block Island pretty well."

"Yes."

At a sharp bend in the road, Ginny pointed to a dirt track,

hardly wider than a footpath, that went off between walls of head-high bushes. "Take that."

Lee turned onto it. The Ford jounced along on the sandy soil. The branches on either side were so close they brushed the sides of the car.

"I hope we don't meet anyone coming the other way," Lee said.

"We won't," said Ginny. The farther they had driven from the course the quieter she had gotten, shrinking into herself. Lee too was quiet; she didn't know what to say. On the one hand, her heart went out to Ginny. Maybe they had been deeply in love, maybe Ginny had felt for Stuart what Lee felt for Graham. Why not? Stuart had been charming, pleasant, kind. And now he was dead. Murdered. What if their situations had been reversed? What if it were Graham who . . . who . . .

"A left here," Ginny said, as they came to a second dirt road that cut across the first.

On the other hand, there was a part of Lee, some sanctimonious, stiff-necked inner self that she hadn't even known she possessed, that felt little in the way of compassion, let alone empathy, for Ginny. Stuart had been married, after all, and the fact that his wife had been the awful Darlene didn't make any difference. If he and Ginny had wanted a life of their own, why hadn't they made one? Why hadn't Stuart gotten a divorce? Because Darlene would have taken him to the cleaners? No doubt she would have, but in Lee's mind that wasn't reason enough.

Instead, they had carried out their affair behind Darlene's back. No, worse; right in front of her and in front of the people who knew her. And that kind of indifference to another human being's feelings (even Darlene's) was unforgivable.

Lee smiled faintly as these uncharacteristic reflections bounced around in her mind. Could it be that Graham wasn't the only prude around here?

"Here we are," Ginny said.

She stopped the car and they got out. The wind had picked up, and a thin, wispy veil of cloud had come from nowhere to cover the sky. They were on the Mohegan Bluffs, not far from where Lee and Peg had bicycled. A narrow dirt path, possibly made by animals, meandered precipitously along the rim. Ginny walked out onto it for about twenty yards and stopped, staring out to sea. Lee, careful of her footing, followed.

"It's beautiful, Ginny," she said.

It wasn't. It was big, a seascape that stretched to a cloudy, blue-gray horizon in three directions. And it was impressive, with two hundred feet of dark cliffside falling away directly beneath their feet—a little too close for comfort, really—down to a rough, rocky beach and a restless surf. But beautiful it wasn't.

Sinister was more like it; ominous, unsettling. All along the shore, pewter-colored waves seemingly moving in every direction dashed against sharp, glistening, black rocks. And from this height, they could see other rocks below the surface, where they would be invisible to boats, but nonetheless deadly. On the beach below, not far to Lee's left, was the derelict, shattered half of a wooden boat, a commercial one, perhaps a fishing boat, with a loading hatch set into the splintered deck. The blackened struts of the boat's frame were exposed, for all the world like a set of flayed human ribs, and a broken mast, as big around as a telephone pole, lay at a crazy angle across what was left of the stove-in hull. Other than this ruined hulk and some warning buoys that bobbed a few hundred yards out, there was nothing in the vast marine scene before them that suggested intelligent life on earth. They might have been on some barren volcanic island a thousand miles out in the Atlantic. A shivery chill wriggled its way down between Lee's shoulders.

"I wouldn't call it beautiful," Ginny said bleakly. "Do you know where we are?"

Lee shook her head.

"The southwest corner of the island. This is Black Rock Point."

"Good name for it," Lee said. She'd heard of it, probably from Peg or Benny. "Ginny," she began, searching for the right words, "I just want to say . . . I mean, I know how you must feel—"

"Do you?" Ginny said curtly.

Well, Lee had deserved that; it had been a dumb thing to say. "I mean, I know how close you and Stuart were, so—"

Ginny turned on her. "You don't know anything! You don't know a damn thing!"

Now, *that* she hadn't deserved. She quashed a prickle of temper. It wasn't *her* idea to be standing out on this desolate, windswept, godforsaken point. If she'd had her druthers she'd still be nudging those clean, white balls on that lush, green surface, improving her game, not fruitlessly trying to console this grieving, edgy woman. All the same, it was impossible for Lee not to feel in her own chest at least a dull, pale echo of the heartache Ginny was going through.

"Look, Ginny," she said gently, "I know I can't really grasp what it must be like for you, but I *do* know what I feel for Graham, and it isn't as hard as you think for me to imagine how *I'd* feel it . . . well, if something happened—"

Ginny was peering at her as if she thought she couldn't believe her ears. "What you feel for *Graham?*"

"Yes—"

"And you think that's what I felt for Stuart?"

"Well, not exactly, of course," Lee said, floundering, not sure what the miscommunication was. "No two relationships can be the same, but—"

"You think he was my *lover*? Is that what you think?"

"Well—yes."

"Where did you ever get an idea like that?"

Now she was thoroughly flustered. "I don't know—I heard—I thought—I'm not sure, I must have just assumed—I must have noticed that you seemed close, so I just, I mean I just . . ." When she finally ran out of blather she just stood there and waited for Ginny to say something. It took a while. Ginny turned away and stared out to sea again for almost a minute.

"I loved him, yes, but, my God, not that way," she said at last, still looking at the horizon. "Stuart was like my father. We were like father and daughter."

"I see," Lee said. *Do* I see? She wondered.

"Lee," Ginny said in a faraway voice, "is that what they all think? That Stuart and I were having an affair?"

"I . . ." She wanted to say no, that she had no idea what the others thought or didn't think, but the lie stuck in her throat. "At least one of them, yes," she said.

Ginny turned to her again. She was perfectly composed now, almost serene. "Lee, do you know what happened here in 1971? At Black Rock Point?"

Lee shook her head.

Ginny drew a long, slow breath, as if she were collecting herself for a long story. "There was an old wreck—"

"Of course!" Lee exclaimed, suddenly remembering why Black Rock Point sounded familiar. "The *Good Hope*! This is where it went down."

"Yes. And do you know the rest of the story?"

"Yes, Benny told me all about it today. Stuart and Benny and another man—"

"Andy Gottlieb," Ginny said.

"That's right. They were partners, they had a converted lobster boat—"

"The *Virginia II.*"

"That was it, yes. Gottlieb was killed the day they—" Lee
stopped as a strange, impossible idea formed in her mind. The
Virginia II . . . The chill returned, this time crawling upward, up
the nape of her neck and into her skull. She could feel the individual hairs stand up.

"It happened just beyond that buoy over there," Ginny said
softly. "Most of the wreck's still out there, did you know that?"

"No, I didn't. Ginny—"

"Stuart felt awful about it. Did you know he gave thirty thousand dollars to Andy's wife and little girl?"

"Ginny, the boat, the *Virginia II*—"

Ginny smiled. "Yes. It was named for me. I was born Virginia
Gottlieb."

"Then—"

She nodded. "That's right, I'm the little girl. Andy Gottlieb
was my father."

✳   ✳   ✳

The rest of the story came out on the drive back to
Quonochaugachaug. Stuart, it seemed, had not only given
$30,000 to Andy's family, he had willingly taken on a sincere
sense of responsibility for the future of ten-year-old Ginny
Gottlieb. Although he had never contacted her personally, a few
years later he had put more money into a trust for her education
and eventually overseen her M.B.A. in managerial accounting
from a discreet distance. When Ginny married a much older
man named Boz Briggs in 1987, Stuart had dropped out of the
picture, but after Briggs died of a stoke in 1991, Stuart reen-
tered her life, offering her a job as payroll supervisor at SRS.

Ginny was understandably torn. She knew that Stuart was the man that had paid for her education and helped her and her mother in countless ways over the years. She also knew that he was the man that had picked up a knife and personally, purposefully cut her father's lifeline, leaving him to die on the ocean floor. After a week's indecision, however, she accepted the offer on two conditions: first, that no one know that she was Gottlieb's daughter, and second, that Stuart treat her no differently from any other employee. If she was going to succeed she was adamant that it be on her own merit.

The first condition was fulfilled to the letter; the second wasn't so easy. A genuine attachment flowered between them. Ginny was the daughter Stuart had never had, and Stuart warmly took the place of Ginny's own dimly remembered father. Two years later—strictly on merit, as Ginny told it—she was promoted to financial manager, where she revolutionized the company's financial base and methods, greatly improving their tax position and cash-flow situation.

Stuart had been both boss and father to her, her work had been immensely satisfying, and, aside from Darlene's continuing antipathy (Darlene alone knew who she was and had immediately and enthusiastically cast herself in a role that she was made for: wicked stepmother), these had been the most wonderful years of her life.

"Until yesterday," she said with a sigh as they turned at the Quonochaugachaug Public Golf Course sign and started up the winding driveway. "Everything's topsy-turvy now that he's dead." She shook her head, a single sharp snap. "Dead. That's the first time I've actually said it out loud."

"Ginny, who do you think did this? It almost has to be someone that—"

Ginny put her hands to her ears. "Please, could we not talk

about it? I've tried and tried to think—Bert, Frank, Malcolm—
and it's like my mind just shuts down and won't do it. It's too
horrible. I get numb."

"I'm sorry, Ginny, I shouldn't have asked."

"It's okay. Lee . . . about what I told you before . . . you won't
mention it to the others, will you? I wouldn't want—"

"No, I won't. But have you told the police?"

"The police? No, why should I tell the police?"

"I assume they'd like to hear anything about Stuart's past that
might tie in. Graham's always telling me that you can never tell
where some supposedly insignificant fact might lead."

That was putting it mildly, she thought but didn't say. Couldn't
Ginny see that this wasn't insignificant at all, that it gave her one
heck of a motive for killing Stuart? With his own hands the man
had knowingly severed her father's air hose and caused his death.
Of *course* the police would want to know. And if Ginny didn't
tell them, they'd be even more interested in knowing why she
hadn't.

"Really," Lee said emphatically, "I think you ought—"

Ginny shook her head, also emphatically. "No, I don't see
that it's their business, or anybody's business, who my father was.
I got where I am on my own steam, Lee. My name is Ginny
Briggs, not Ginny Gottlieb. That's not a lie, it's perfectly true,
and it's all anybody has to know."

                    *   *   *

Lee's putting-instruction session was uneventful and less than
sparkling. The truth was, she didn't know what to tell them. The
truth was, she had never really believed you could be taught to
putt, or that there was any one best way to do it, or three best
ways, or even thirty best ways. Oh, there were a few basics: keeping the eyes directly above the ball was generally a good idea, and

so was keeping the putter face properly aligned, but that was it, despite what the conventional wisdom and the scads of instruction manuals had to say.

Even the pros couldn't agree on how to do it right. Generally speaking, professional golfers were in agreement as to what a perfect swing with a driver or a 5-iron ought to look like (Nick Faldo's or Patty Sheehan's, for example), but when it came to putting, they were all over the map. Some of the best (and worst) used smooth, long pendulum strokes, some used wristy taps; some positioned the ball opposite the left foot, some centered it. Some bent from the waist or hips, some didn't. And what worked one year wasn't guaranteed to work the next. Listening to a bunch of topflight professionals gab about putting was no different from listening to a bunch of Sunday hackers. They were forever coming up with new tricks, new keys, new cures, new putters. It was not uncommon for golfers who had stuck with one brand of irons and woods for two decades to own twenty different types of putters—long-handled and short-handled, bladed and mallet-styled, desperately switching from one to another when they mysteriously—and regularly— lost the touch. And more than one well-known pro relied in all seriousness on his or her "lucky" putter. Which told you a lot about the "science" of putting right there.

So Lee used her first twenty minutes trying to get them to keep their eyes over the ball and their club faces aligned, then turned to the difficult art of "reading" the green: determining the land's contours, the grain of the grass, and whatever else might affect the speed of the ball or its break.

"What does that mean, exactly—break?" Ginny asked.

"It's any curve the ball takes as a result of a slope on the green," Lee told her.

"On the putting green, as in life," intoned Bert with the sage cadence of a Zen master, "a nasty break can really spoil your day. Remember this, grasshopper."

Lee and Peg exchanged quick glances. *Well, he sure got that right,* Lee thought. *And then some.*

After that, the only moment of interest came when Peg whispered to her: "Got some curious things to tell you."

"Same here," Lee replied. "I'll talk to you at lunch."

But that was not to be. Malcolm, who had remained back at the inn working, had telephoned Quonochaugachaug to say that he had scheduled a working lunch—sandwiches in the Dory Room—to be followed by an afternoon goal-setting session. He was sorry to interfere with their well-earned relaxation, but there was much to be done.

With heavy-hearted groans they had returned to the inn in two cars, taking Jackie with them and leaving Lee at the practice range with the third car. She got a bucket of balls and worked through them with her fairway woods, less for the sake of practice than for the all-out, free-swinging pleasure of it after an hour of putting with its precise, small-scale movements. Then she drove into town, parked on the main street, and got a takeout hot dog for lunch. She ate standing on the ferry dock, leaning on a railing and watching a Galilee-bound ferry head smoothly northward out of Old Harbor and then begin to pitch and wallow as it cleared the tip of the Lantern Rock breakwater and reached the rougher seas of Block Island Sound.

She made a mental note to pick up some Dramamine at the Seaside Market just up the street before leaving the island. Unless, of course, she flew off to JFK with Graham when it came time to go, which was a strong possibility inasmuch as they would be together here for the weekend. By themselves. This led to a string of pleasant associations that would ordinarily have been enough to occupy her mind while the sausage digested, but not today. She was thinking about Ginny. More specifically, she was thinking about going to Chief Tolliver with what she had learned.

My name is Ginny Briggs, not Ginny Gottlieb, Ginny had said, *and it's all anybody has to know.*

Maybe. Assuming that Ginny hadn't had anything to do with Stuart's death, then who her father was or wasn't was beside the point. The catch lay in that "assuming." Ginny might know that she was innocent, but Lee couldn't know it and neither did anybody else. Somebody at the retreat had murdered Stuart, and Ginny, unlikely as she was, wasn't any more improbable than Jackie or Benny or Darlene (well, maybe a case could be made for Darlene) or Frank or any of them.

Or, wait a minute, perhaps Ginny *was* a little less likely than the rest. Would she have gone out of her way to come over and tell Graham that she'd been walking on the beach with Stuart if she'd just killed him? Pretty doubtful.

All the same, stranger things had happened.

No, the police needed to know, and if Ginny wouldn't tell them, Lee had to.

That was all there was to it.

*   *   *

"New Shoreham Police Department," the sign on the lawn said, with an official-looking triangular emblem beside it to further make the point. Even so, it looked more like a suite of suburban doctors' offices than a police station: a one-story, gray-shingled building at the edge of the village, with white trim, an inviting green lawn in front, and a neatly shaved hedge on either side of the entrance. The lobby looked like a doctor's waiting room too: a neat little space with a glass-fronted reception counter and a couple of plastic chairs for visitors. All it needed were a few two-year-old copies of *Today's Health* and *Gastroenterology Journal* scattered on the surface of the Formica-topped coffee table.

"I'd like to see Chief Tolliver," she said when the diminutive woman behind the counter looked up from her paperwork.

The woman sized her up, not unkindly. "I'm sorry, the chief's unavailable at the moment. May I help you?"

"Well, it's about the murder he's working on—"

As Lee thought it would, that got her attention. "Just a moment." She pressed a button on her telephone, raising her eyes inquiringly to Lee at the same time.

"Lee Ofsted," Lee said in response.

"Arnie," the woman said, wedging the receiver between her ear and her shoulder while she went on working, "there's a Lee Ofsted here to see you about—yes, all right, I will." She put the phone down and pointed at the lobby's single door. "Through the big room and out the back door. Chief's office is in the trailer out back. Just walk in."

Tolliver was stuffing plastic wrap into a paper bag when she came in. An opened can of diet root beer was on his desk, along with a file folder open to some kind of list with penciled check marks next to some of the entries. Still chewing, he waved her into the chair in front of the desk.

"Sorry to interrupt your lunch," Lee said.

"I'm done. Working lunch, anyway." He flipped the bag, basketball-style, into a wastepaper basket six feet away, got out his tobacco pouch, and started on the pipe smoker's long, lazy rigamarole of lighting up. "What can I do for you?"

"How's the investigation coming?" She didn't expect to be told, but it didn't hurt to ask.

"Not bad. Might have some pictures for you to look at in a day or so."

"Pictures?"

"Fella with the wig," he said.

It took her a moment to figure out what he was talking about. Stuart's murder had pushed that bizarre kidnapping attempt into the dim past, like some isolated incident that had happened, or maybe not really happened, decades ago. She counted back. Three days, that was all. The bruise under her eye had barely begun to yellow.

"Why, that's fine," she said. "Just let me know."

"Now, what can I do for you?" he asked again. The worn, gray swivel chair creaked as he leaned back and clasped his hands behind his head. On the wall behind him was a framed photograph of a younger, thinner Chief Tolliver receiving a diploma at the FBI's national police academy.

"I have some information I think you'll be interested in."

He nodded. "Shoot."

She told him about Ginny's being Andy Gottlieb's daughter, drawing it out a bit more than was strictly necessary, just to see if it was possible to get a rise out of the unflappable police chief.

She did, relatively speaking, anyway. He creaked the chair upright, unclasped his hands, and took the pipe out of his mouth.

"Don't that beat all," he said.

Chapter 15

"Mmm."

Lee inhaled the aromas emanating from the white cardboard cartons that she and Peg were laying out on the picnic table. "Good take-out Chinese food on this little island. Who would have thought?"

"Credit human ingenuity and the free-market system," Peg said. "Ah, look, they threw in some fried wonton that we didn't even order. And this must be sweet-and-sour sauce." She applied one to the other, tasted, nodded her approval, and munched away while continuing to open cartons and plastic sauce containers with contagious pleasure. Peg was the happiest eater Lee knew. "Boy, am I glad I thought of this."

"This" was an early dinner shared by just the two of them. Peg, wearying of the rich Continental food at the Mooncussers, had asked Benny if there was a Chinese restaurant on the island. There wasn't, he told her, but she could order from the China Pavilion in Westerly on the mainland, and the restaurant would get it to the Westerly airport in time for the next hourly passenger flight to Block Island. The delivery charge was only five dollars, and since the flight took but twelve minutes, the food would arrive as hot as if it had come in a neighborhood delivery truck.

And so it was. The food was still steaming as they started in on it with paper plates and plastic utensils (Lee's contribution, along with cans of ginger ale, from the Seaside Market on Water Street). They had driven up Center Road from the airport, then out Beach Avenue to the yacht basin on the west side of the island and taken possession of one of the picnic tables overlooking the marina at New Harbor, dense with the swaying masts of visiting yachts of every shape and size. The water was blue, the air was fresh, and the clank of anchor chains mixed agreeably with the background sounds of seagulls and people. For a while they concentrated happily on the food: vegetable rolls, barbecued spareribs, chicken with snow peas, seafood lo mein, steamed rice.

Lee was a pretty good trencherman herself, so they were spooning out second helpings before the talk got any more complicated than "yum," "ah," and "try some of this."

"Ginny is Andy Gottlieb's daughter," Lee said without preamble.

Peg's reaction was considerably more rewarding than Chief Tolliver's had been. The forkful of chicken and snow peas that was three-quarters of the way to her lips was lowered slowly back to her plate. Her mouth, opened to receive it, stayed that way for some seconds before she closed it. "Ginny . . . Andy Gottlieb . . . you gotta be . . . how did you . . ."

"The *Virginia II* was named for her," Lee said, and filled Peg in on the rest of the story, midway through which Peg remembered to resume eating.

"And nobody knows all this?" Peg asked when Lee had finished.

Lee shook her head. "Nobody at SRS."

"What about the police? That's something they ought to know. Do you think they do?"

"They do now. I spent half an hour in Tolliver's office telling him." She hunched her shoulders. "I feel a little funny about it. Ginny's really sensitive about not wanting people to think she's gotten where she has because of any special consideration from Stuart. She made me promise not to say anything to anyone at SRS."

"Well, you didn't. Tolliver's not at SRS."

"Yes, but she *meant* anyone at all. I tried to get her to go to the police herself, but she just—"

"Stop worrying about it, hon," Peg said. "You did the right thing. Of course they had to know something like that. Look, for all we know, Ginny's the one who killed him."

"I know, but I can't really make myself believe—"

"Neither can I, but what do we know? *Somebody* did. Pass the noodles, will you? Now, I have news too. Wait'll you hear about Frank Wishniak."

"Don't tell me, let me guess," Lee said. "He's Andy Gottlieb's brother-in-law?"

"No, but just as interesting. Frank—um, there wouldn't be any more spareribs left, would there?"

Frank Wishniak and Stuart Chappell, she told Lee as she re-stocked her plate, went back over twenty-five years, almost as far as Stuart, Benny, and Andy had. After Andy had been killed and Stuart had bought out Benny's interest in the *Good Hope*, Stuart, the least experienced salvage diver of the original threesome, had gone looking for expert assistance to raise the hoped-for treasure. He had settled on Frank, then thirty-five, an ex-navy frogman and an underwater welder and senior diver at the General Dynamics shipyard in New London. Frank took a month to carefully study the situation off Black Rock Point and then laid out a detailed operational plan for safely recovering the vessel's contents. With Stuart's approval he hired four temporary divers to work under his supervision, and the resulting smooth, successful operation, as everyone now knew, had made Stuart a small fortune and provided him with the money to launch SRS.

"What do you think of *that*?" Peg said proudly. "It's Frank who actually did all the work. And Frank was the one who first recognized that those spikes were something special, or at least that's the way he tells it."

Lee thought all this over before responding. "Don't that beat all," she said, bringing a peculiar look from Peg.

"Anyway," Peg went on, "Stuart was grateful enough to give him a five-thousand-dollar bonus."

"Five thousand dollars," Lee mused. "Out of the two hundred thousand-plus that Frank made for him. Would that be likely to make somebody grateful or resentful?"

"Good question. How would you feel?"

"Both," Lee said after a moment. "Grateful at first, then maybe more and more resentful as the years passed and I had time to mull it over."

Peg nodded. "Indeed, especially if you found yourself still working for Stuart as a hired hand when you were sixty years old, and you knew in your heart that you knew more about underwater salvage than Stuart and everybody else at SRS put together, even if you didn't have a college degree, and that you, Stuart's oldest, most loyal employee, had just been passed over for promotion in favor of a smarmy young Johnny-come-lately who knew more about strategic subsystem parameters than he did about which end of a ship was aft."

Lee looked at her. "And you're saying that's the way Frank feels? Betrayed?"

"Well, Frank's a pretty jolly sort, as you know. From the way he acts you'd say he was happy as a clam. But reading between the lines, yes, I'd say that's the way he feels."

"That's an awful lot to read between the lines," Lee said doubtfully.

"I'm pretty good at that sort of thing, Lee."

Lee laughed. "I can vouch for that." She was starting to get full now, and had begun to spear the bite-sized bits of meat and vegetable on her plate, leaving the noodles and rice behind. "So that gives us two people who might have had love-hate relationships with Stuart: Ginny and Frank. And both of them have a connection to the *Good Hope.* I'm not suggesting either of them *did* kill Stuart, but if they did—"

"Then that horrible bit with the spike might have seemed like some kind of perverted justice to them." She shuddered. "Brr."

"We better make that three people," Lee said. "Bert may not have had a love relationship with Stuart, but there was sure a hate relationship." She smiled faintly. "I can read between the lines too, if the writing is big enough."

"But Bert has no connection to the *Good Hope.* What would the spike mean to him?"

"Plenty. He's Benny's nephew, isn't he?"

Peg stared at her. "*Is* he?"

"Of course, don't you remember . . . oops, I found that out yesterday. Did I forget to tell you?"

"I think maybe you did." Peg shook her head wonderingly. "You know, I'm beginning to understand why the lines of authority at SRS were in such a mess. The damn thing is practically a family business. You'd think Stuart would have let me in on all this, wouldn't you?"

"And in Bert's opinion," Lee continued, mining her own vein, "Stuart took advantage of Benny—'screwed him over royally' was the way he put it—and, who knows, maybe he's wanted to get even in his behalf all these years. Or maybe he figures that if Benny had a lot of money, *he'd* have been in line to inherit it. Either way, there's a connection to the *Good Hope*."

"True. And while we're at it, by the way, we might as well add Benny to the list too. He had plenty of reason to resent Stuart's success."

Lee laughed. "Maybe it'd be easier to come up with a list of people who didn't have any reason to murder anybody."

"It'd be shorter anyway," said Peg. "It's exactly one person long. Malcolm's the only one of the managers who doesn't go back to the *Good Hope* one way or another."

"As far as we're aware," Lee corrected. "If anyone had asked us yesterday, we'd have said *none* of them had any connection. For all we know, Malcolm is Paul Revere's great-great-great-grandson."

"You're sure right about that."

"And what about Darlene, while we're thinking about likely murderers? Were she and Stuart married back then?"

Peg shook her head. "No, she's his second wife. I forget exactly when they got married, but it was long after the *Good Hope* affair. She used to be a clothes model for golf outfits, and she and Stuart met at some kind of pre-tournament fund-raiser—oh, ten or fifteen years ago, so there's no connection to the wreck." She scooped up a last mouthful of rice and pushed her plate away. "At the same time . . ." She drifted off, still chewing, eyes on the horizon.

"Yes?" Lee said. "Are you planning on letting me in on this?"

"Oh, sorry. I was just thinking. Let's forget about the *Good Hope* for a minute. When Stuart hired me, the first thing I did was go into my Internet chat groups and bulletin boards—and I'm in a lot of them—and see if there was any interesting gossip about him."

"Well, naturally. What else would a good management consultant do first?"

Peg looked icily down her nose at Lee. "It is always of value,"
she said grandly, "to make an initial assessment of the psy-
chosocial subsystem and interactive process determinants before
beginning any organizational analysis."

"I sincerely apologize," Lee said. "Chalk it up to ignorance.
So what kind of gossip did you dig up? Pardon me—what kind
of interactive process determinants?"

"Some pretty juicy ones, actually," Peg said, smiling her dimple-
cheeked smile. "Apparently Darlene was a top model, a real
knockout in those days—"

"I can believe that."

"—and a real party girl too, if you get my drift. After they
got married she kept working, and she was pretty popular on the
golf circuit. Stuart would be off coordinating some salvage proj-
ect in the Caspian Sea and Darlene would be knocking them out
in Phoenix or Atlanta, at some high-society affair. I guess there
was some deliciously notorious behavior at the Wheatix Open
in 1991; Darlene supposedly had a fling with one of the big-
name pros—"

"Really? Who?"

Peg shrugged. "God, I wish I knew, but I could *not* come up
with a name. Believe me, I tried."

"I don't doubt it."

"Look, I don't even know if it's true. We're deep in rumor
country now, you understand. Anyway, the story is they
wound up skinny-dipping at midnight in the country club
swimming pool, and that they had to pay somebody hush
money to keep it quiet, and that it wasn't just a one-night affair either, but—"

"Peg, this is interesting, but I don't see—"

"The thing is, rumor or not, it must have gotten back to Stuart because that was it. No more modeling, no more fooling around on her own at tournaments. If Stuart didn't go, she didn't go."

"I still don't—"

"The only point I'm making is that we are not talking about a marriage made in heaven here. Darlene may very well have wanted out, and Stuart may have refused, at least on her terms, and isn't it just possible that Darlene—"

"What? Arranged to have herself kidnapped? Then changed her mind and fought her way out of it? Then—"

Peg sighed. "All right, all right. I guess it doesn't sound too probable when you put it like that."

Lee spotted a last scallop under some noodles and fished it out. "When you figure in the kidnapping, nothing sounds too probable. I mean, if the idea was ransom in the first place, then why go through the horrible rigmarole with the spike later? And if the idea was revenge over the *Good Hope* affair, then why the ransom attempt? They just don't go together."

"Maybe they don't," Peg said. "Maybe they're two completely different things that don't have anything to do with each other." At Lee's look she added: "Well, it *is* possible."

Lee shook her head. "No, they're related. Stuart knew who was behind it. He said so. He was killed to keep him from telling." She stiffened, trying to keep the thought from coming, but it came anyway. Again. *And I'm the one responsible for his dying.*

"Damn," she said softly.

Peg, knowing what she was thinking, busied herself with gathering up the emptied cartons and stuffing them into the bag, and after a moment Lee joined her.

"Let's see, is there anybody we haven't libeled?" Peg asked

brightly as they opened an overlooked waxed-paper bag containing two fortune cookies.

"Well, we really haven't come up with anything against Malcolm."

"No, but I really think Malcolm's in the clear. Whatever his reasons, why in the world would he kill Stuart now of all times? He just got promoted to veep. In fact, why would he want to kill Stuart at all? If Stuart has gone and left SRS to Darlene, which he probably has, I'd say Malcolm's in big trouble. There's bad blood there. No, he was better off with Stuart alive and running things."

"Okay, how about Jackie?"

"Jackie? What do we have on Jackie?"

"Nothing that comes to mind," Lee said, "but I bet we could think of something if we put our minds to it."

Peg wrinkled her nose. "It'd be pretty hard. Jackie's an independent contractor, a week in, and then out. Why should it matter to him who lives or dies at SRS—as long as he gets paid?" She glanced at her watch. "I'm going to have to get back, Lee. Malcolm's scheduled a working dinner—not that I'm going to want any dinner—and then an evening work session to follow." She puffed out her cheeks. "Whoo, things have changed at SRS. What's your fortune cookie say?"

Lee broke it open. A little happy-face on the slip smiled up at her. " 'When it is dark,' " she read aloud, " 'all cats are gray.' That sums things up pretty well, wouldn't you say? What do you have?"

" 'A fool will ask more questions in an hour than a wise man can answer in seven years,' " Peg read, and chuckled. "Now, why didn't we open that in the first place and save ourselves all that heavy-duty brainwork?"

Chapter 16

When it is dark, all cats are gray. Now, there was one fortune cookie that knew what it was talking about.

Musing on one gray cat or another, Lee tossed aside a *Golf Digest* that she had picked up at the Book Nook on Water Street a couple of hours earlier, during a stroll down the hill and into town to walk off some of those spareribs. She had been leafing through it while waiting for Graham's promised call from Toronto but gave up when she realized she was just turning the pages, her mind elsewhere. Now, lying back against propped-up pillows on the bed, her shoes off, her arms clasped around her knees, she gave herself over to what was bothering her.

There were two things, and she needed Graham's input on both of them. One she could easily ask him about. The other wasn't going to be so simple to bring up—assuming she wanted to bring it up, which she wasn't sure she did. Which meant it was pretty unlikely to get resolved.

She sighed and looked at her watch for the third time since seven o'clock. Seven-twelve. You'd think he would have called by now; he must have finished up his consulting hours ago.

She fixed the telephone with a baleful eye. *Ring, darn you.*

It worked; the phone rang. She was off the bed and beside it before the sound died away, but on second thought she let it chirp twice more. No point in having him think she had nothing better to do than sit around and wait for his call.

"Hi," she said.

"Hi, yourself. Sorry, this is not Graham," Peg said.

"I—what makes you think I thought it was?"

"Are you kidding? You sure wouldn't say 'hi' like that to me."

"Like what? I just said 'hi.' Can't a person say 'hi'? How am I supposed to say 'hi'?"

"Are you interested in finding out why I'm calling," Peg inquired patiently, "or would you rather continue going through your stock of defense mechanisms?"

Lee laughed and dropped into a chair. "What's up, Peg?"

"I just wasn't sure if anybody told you that there won't be any golf instruction tomorrow morning either. We're having, God help us, another work session."

"Not tomorrow either? But it's the last day."

"I know. Jackie's talked Malcolm into having a wrap-up out at the range at four P.M., but that's it. From now till then, it's all work, no play. I think Malcolm is working at perfecting his Simon Legree leadership mode. Sigh."

"Poor Peg. Are the sessions going well, at least?"

"Actually, yes. And I can hardly complain. They *are* paying me quite a lot, after all." After a moment she said: "Of course they're paying you too—quite a lot—but *you're* going to get another day off. What are you going to do with yourself, practice?"

"Sleep in, to start," Lee said, already looking forward to it. "Then I'll see."

Once Peg had hung up, Lee went ahead and punched in the number of Graham's cell phone. If she wanted to talk to him there was no reason why she couldn't call him for a change. As

Peg had implied, she was rolling in dough, at least for the moment.

Unlike Lee, Graham wasn't coy about picking up his telephone. He answered on the first ring, which probably meant the phone was in his pocket and he was somewhere other than his hotel room.

"Did I call you at a bad time?" she asked. "I can—"

"Lee! *Hi!*"

The ready affection in his voice was enough to get a warm glow going in her chest. If Lee said "hi" when she thought she was talking to him the way he said "hi" when he was talking to her, then no wonder Peg had seen right through her.

"It's never a bad time for you to call," he went deliciously on, "but I probably won't be able to talk very long. I'm about to go off to dinner with the training director to hash a few things over, but at the moment I'm just sitting here while they wrap up some business things on their own. Everything all right there? You keeping out of trouble?"

Lee smiled. "Of course. We're all trying to go on doing things as if everything's normal, but naturally everybody's a little on edge."

"Sure, that's only normal. Have you found out anything new? Has Tolliver let out any information?"

Hm, this was going to require a little thought. Those were two different questions and they had two different answers. *Has Tolliver let out any information?* That was simple: no. *Have you found out anything new?* Well, only that Frank dated back to the *Good Hope* days and had in fact been the man responsible for bringing up the treasure and recognizing the value of the Paul Revere spikes, and that his reward had been a $5,000 bonus and a lifetime job as Stuart's underling. Oh, and also that Ginny Gottlieb just happened to be the daughter of Andy

Gottlieb, the trapped, doomed diver whose air hose Stuart had cut. Other than a few little tidbits like that, no, she hadn't found out anything new.

"Um, not much," she said airily, knowing well enough that Graham would not have been pleased to hear that she and Peg had been busy pumping people for information.

But Graham knew every nuance of her voice. "What do you mean, not *much?*" he demanded, and she could almost see his left eyebrow go up, which was one of *his* nuances and usually meant skepticism or outright suspicion.

Time to change the subject and bring up one of the two things that had been bothering her. "Graham, there's something I want to ask you about. Remember at breakfast yesterday, when you said you thought Darlene's life had been in danger and that she probably would have been killed if that guy had succeeded in getting her?"

"Yes. I still think so. Otherwise he'd never have let her see what he looked like."

"Well, then, why did he bother wearing a wig?"

"Probably to disguise himself from a distance, just in case the people she was playing with caught a glimpse of him. Remember, he thought you and Ginny and Frank were all back at the tee, a hundred and fifty yards away. You weren't supposed to see his face—just that mop of black hair. If you saw him at all."

"Mm." That made sense. On the other hand, it also fit in with the bizarre scenario that had been taking form in her mind ever since her talk with Peg. "Graham, isn't it just possible that he didn't try to disguise himself from Darlene because she already knew what he looked like?"

"I don't follow you. You mean that he was somebody she knew? In that case he'd be *especially*—"

"I mean that she knew what he looked like"—Lee took a

breath and dived in—"because it was all prearranged. Because the whole thing was a fake. Because Darlene was in on the so-called kidnapping from the beginning."

"In on the—but you said she fought like a demon."

"Yes, once I got there. What else could she do?"

"But she was yelling *before* you got there. Yelling and trying to get away from him."

"Yes, for show. As you said, I was supposed to be with the others, way back at the tee, not anywhere where I could reach them in time to interfere."

He was silent for a moment. "But then, later, when he ran, she was screaming at you to get the license plate number," he said finally. "If she didn't want him caught, she'd never have done that."

"Sure, she would have, if she already knew that it was a stolen plate. Or maybe she knew that there wasn't any license plate on the back at all, who knows? Besides, if she wanted the number so much, why didn't she get it herself?" Lee was making it up as she went along now, but it was still holding together as far as she could see.

"Lee, it's too fantastic—"

"Graham, there was only that one thug, and he wasn't even armed, or at least I never saw any kind of weapon. Does that make sense? Wouldn't there have been at least two of them if they were after her for real? How was he going to keep her quiet in the truck while he was driving?"

"Okay, there you have a point. I thought about that too, and my conclusion was that either he was planning to kill her right there, before he drove away—"

"With his bare hands? It's possible, of course, but you'd think—"

"—or else that he had handcuffs with him or some other kind of restraint, or maybe a hypodermic with a sedative in it—"

"Now who's getting fantastic?"

"But it isn't fantastic. You think that sort of thing doesn't happen? Just last March—"

But Lee was in high gear now. "Graham, do you remember how surprised you were when I told you she went out and played golf the very next day? On the very same course? You told me that kind of pointless bravery didn't make any sense, psychologically speaking—"

"Wait a minute, I don't think I ever said—"

But by now she knew she was on a roll and she kept the pressure on. "How much bravery would it have taken if she knew perfectly well there wouldn't be any second attempt on her, because there never really was a first one?"

He breathed in and out twice before answering; two thoughtful, drawn-out breaths. "Well, I suppose that what you're saying makes a certain amount of sense."

"A *certain* amount? It makes more sense than anything anybody else has come up with." Not that anybody else had come up with anything.

"Does it? Where's the motive? Why would she kidnap herself?"

"Obviously, for the money."

"Well, maybe, but that's an approach I never heard of before. A wife collecting ransom money from her husband. How did she expect to spend it without his knowing about it?"

"Well, I don't—"

"And why murder him after it didn't work out?"

"Because he found out about it. He told me he knew who was behind it, didn't he? And now that I think about it, *he* said it was a little 'awkward' too. Doesn't that suggest—"

"And you think she resorted to murder over that? Isn't that a little drastic?"

"Not necessarily—"

"All right, why stab him with the damn spike, tell me that. Do you realize how much extra risk that added? It had to take twenty, thirty seconds to do it. That's a long, dangerous time to hang around somebody you just killed. How could she know someone wouldn't come along while she was doing it? And what could the spike mean to Darlene anyway? She didn't even know him back then, did she?"

But Lee was ready for him. "As a matter of fact, I've been sitting here giving that a lot of thought. Isn't it possible that everybody's been looking in exactly the wrong direction? Maybe the police should have been concentrating on the people for whom the spike *doesn't* mean anything. Couldn't it be a, what do you call it, a false clue, a red herring—something that was purposely done to mislead everyone?"

"It's a thought," Graham said.

And a pretty darn good one, Lee thought. "I mean, when you think about it, revenge is all very well, but why would anybody in their right mind leave the police an obvious, honest-to-God clue pointing right to them?"

Graham was silent for a few seconds. "So you think the spike was just Darlene's way of focusing Tolliver's attention away from her? That's your theory?"

"Yes," she said, not much liking his tone. "That's my theory."

"And what about that peculiar ransom amount? What's your theory on that? What's that supposed to mean?"

"I don't know what it's supposed to mean," Lee snapped. "Do I have to have an answer for everything? All I'm doing is raising what seems to me like at least an outside possibility, and all you're doing is contradicting me, and dismissing everything I say—"

"But I'm not dismissing it," he said quietly.

"—and poking holes in every little—you're not?"

"Absolutely not. I think you're making a hell of a good point."

"But then why were you—"

"Because that's the way my mind works. Also, it's fun to get you stirred up."

"Fun for you, maybe," she said, laughing, "but I'm glad you think I'm onto something."

"Well, at least it's worth exploring. You haven't raised it with Darlene herself, have you? Even in your own subtle way?"

"No, how could I? She's back in Boston. Chief Tolliver let her go back to arrange family affairs, remember?"

"Oh, that's right. Good. Listen, are you going to talk to the chief about this?"

"Yes, don't you think I should?"

"That's exactly what I think you should do. Tell Tolliver what you've been thinking and let him take it from there. Lee, I know you're tired of hearing me say this, but I want you to promise— uh-oh, it looks like the training director's finishing up in the other room."

"That's all right, I know what you were about to say anyway. And, yes, I absolutely promise to stay out of trouble."

Graham laughed. "Fine. I still have a minute; they're chatting at the door. I'm beat, to tell you the truth. I'm glad I'll be having dinner with her at Benihana, right here in our hotel."

Her. Our hotel. How cozy, how too-too charming.

And there it was, problem number two, the one that wasn't so easy to talk to him about or even to think about. To put it bluntly, Lee was jealous, increasingly so, and it wasn't an emotion

that she had much prior experience with. It just wasn't in her na-
ture, or so she'd thought before her steady, reliable—and even
predictable—Carmel detective lieutenant had taken to jetting
around the world and eating in Benihanas with smart, seductive
training directors who no doubt looked (and acted?) like Sharon
Stone. And sharing hotels with them.

"Well, enjoy yourself," she said, then added what she thought
was an offhanded: "What's she like?"

"Dark hair, nice-looking, intelligent, about thirty-five," he
said crisply. "Also happily married, with two children and a nice
guy for a husband, who'll be joining us later for coffee and
dessert. I believe that's what you wanted to know?"

"Graham, I'm sorry, I didn't mean to sound . . . however I
sounded. I guess I'm a little—insecure."

"Insecure?" He sounded genuinely surprised. "You mean
about me? Are you kidding? I'm the one who's worried. There
you are out all by yourself and unattached on that crazy golf
tour—TV people, parties, sexy athletes, celebrities on the
prowl—"

"Graham, believe me, you have nothing to worry about."

"Well, neither do you. I'm afraid you're stuck with me."

"Well, then." She steeled herself and plunged in without letting herself think about what she was doing. "Why don't we
make it official?" she said rapidly, before she could change her
mind. "How about getting engaged?"

But even while she was saying it, she heard him speaking to
someone else, his voice muffled by his hand over the speaker.

"Oh, hell, I'm going to have to go," he said to her a moment
later. "What were you saying?"

"I—nothing important. It'll hold."

"All right, I'll give you a call later, when I get in."

"No, don't. The last thing I want is for you to be calling me

because you think you *should.* I'm fine, believe me. Go enjoy yourself. I'm not worried anymore, it was just a momentary lapse."

Nothing at all, really; only about seven months long. And
now, when she'd finally gotten up her nerve to say something
about it, he'd been talking to somebody else.

"Well, I'll call you tomorrow, then. Oh—there's a possibility
we might finish up in the morning. If we do, and I hustle, I
might be able to get back to Block Island tomorrow afternoon
instead of the next day. Would that be okay?"

She smiled. "I wouldn't say no."

*   *   *

"Oh, my aching back," Peg said, meaning it literally and sincerely. She glared at the open laptop computer on the table,
stretched, kneaded the muscles in her neck, and got up to brew
another pot of super-strong French roast in the portable
espresso maker she took with her on business trips for times like
this. A nice, neat little gadget with its own cup and built-in containers for sugar, creamer, and a quarter-pound of fine-ground
Starbucks. Sometimes the caffeine did the trick, sometimes not.

So far tonight: not even close.

While the coffee brewed and her muscles unkinked she stood
at the open window—the wind off the sea took care of the
mosquitoes—and stared out at a velvety sky with a few pale
stars, and at an ocean invisible except for a milky shimmer along
the horizon. The steady pounding of the surf a quarter of a
mile away was in its late-night mode, booming and hollow.

It was 1:15 A.M. and she'd been at the computer for almost
three solid hours, with nothing to show for it except a growing
pile of petered-out leads. When she first sat down she'd been
certain the answer lay in the Dow-Jones average, and for over an
hour she had tried one calculation after another: with dividends

reinvested, without dividends reinvested, you name it. Results: zilch.

She'd tried the same thing and gotten the same results with the Standard & Poor's 500. Then, after a call to a friend who worked for the Bureau of Labor Statistics, she'd applied the latest gross domestic product deflator to all the earlier calculations, and had gotten nothing for her trouble but a steadily increasing backache.

The strangling sounds that indicated that the espresso maker was finishing up brought her from the window to pour herself a cup and she went wearily back to the armchair and the laptop. For ten minutes she glowered at it and took an occasional sip of coffee, waiting for ideas. Nothing happened. Finally she dug her address book out of her handbag and dialed a number in Seattle, Washington, where the time was not quite 10:30. Late but not that late. She hoped.

The phone was picked up on the third ring. "Yes?"

"Professor? This is Peg Fiske? Formerly Peggy Barber? Remember me?"

"How could I forget," was the flatly delivered response, best not pursued. Professor Eugene Silberberg, now retired, had been Peg's economics professor at the otherwise second-rate (but expensive) university she'd attended, and although he was famously crotchety, he was a kind enough old geezer at heart, and he had been helpful to her more than once over the years.

"I'm sorry to be calling so late—"

"That's quite all right," he said. "I was merely sleeping."

Peg smiled. Same old prof. "—but I have a question on economics that I'm hoping you can help me with."

"Yes?" She heard the quickening of interest.

"I'm trying to figure out how much money—"

"Economics," he interrupted tartly, "is not about money."

Amazing man. Twenty seconds out of sleep and here came the opening lecture from Principles of Microeconomics, as lively as it had been the first (and second and third) times she'd heard it. "Economics is a science, my dear woman, a *social* science that seeks explanations—"

—*of events that take place in the real world through the analysis of human behavior*, Peg thought to herself on a wave of nostalgia. She waited for him to complete the sentence, which he did, word for word, and then told him what her problem was and how she'd gone about trying to solve it.

"And what did you get when you tried the CPI?" he asked.

"The CPI?"

"The Consumer Price—"

"I remember what it is, sir, it just didn't occur to me to use it."

"Well, I don't see why not. I'd have begun with it. Here, just a moment." The telephone clattered on a hard surface, to be followed by mutters and rustling paper. "Here. The CPI in 1971 was 40.5. Now, if I were you I'd start by using the latest average annual CPI."

"I will. I'll call BLS first thing in the morning and—"

"No, no, no," he said, "I have it here somewhere. You'd be surprised how useful it is to have around." More mutters, more rustles, continuing for some time. "Here we are," he said at last into the telephone. "One-fifty-two-point-four."

"One-fifty-two-point-four," Peg said, writing it down. "Thanks a million, Prof."

"But do you know what to do with it?" he asked. "That would seem to be the critical point."

"I think I do." She told him what she had in mind.

"That should work," he allowed. "Well, good luck, then. Let me know how it comes out."

"I certainly will."

The telephone was almost back on its hook when she heard a squawk from it. She put it back to her ear. "Sir? Did you say something?"

"In the *morning*," he said.

Eagerly she turned back to the computer. The formula was simple enough: $40.5/152.4 \times 650{,}993$. She hit *Enter*, then closed her eyes. "Come on," she urged the numbers, "give me a break." She opened her right eye to peek, and then the left, to make sure she'd read it right.

She had.

Bingo.

*   *   *

True to her word to Peg, Lee slept late the next morning, never hearing the hubbub of the others bustling down to breakfast. Too bad, because she had wanted to chat with Peg about her latest thoughts on Darlene, but by the time she got out of bed it was a quarter to nine; by the time she finished dressing it was nine-thirty and Peg and the others were off at their meeting. Lee called the police department from her room and spoke to the same receptionist she'd talked to before. The chief was in, Lee was informed, and would continue to be in all morning, and probably all afternoon for that matter, and Lee could come in to talk with him anytime.

As she went downstairs she was beginning to have second thoughts about Chief Tolliver and his sleepy, let-things-take-their-course approach to crime fighting. What was he doing sitting around his office all day? Why wasn't he out catching the murderer? He and his tall sergeant had shown up around the inn once or twice after Stuart's death, talking to one person or another, but mostly they had been strictly low-profile. It was start-

ing to seem like a good thing Lee was doing some of their thinking for them.

Breakfast was long over, with the waitress just finishing mop-
ping up, but Benny was nice about getting her some coffee and
warming up one of the sticky buns Jackie was so fond of. The
thing was actually too gluey for Lee's taste, but she didn't have
the heart to turn him down, and she dutifully finished it off on
the front porch while he sat in one of the rocking chairs and
beamed kindly at her from over a mug of coffee of his own; he
was a natural innkeeper, the kind of person who enjoyed watching other people eat.

Lee chewed away and smiled back at him, but not as whole-
heartedly as she once had. He had made a show of telling her
everything there was to tell about himself and Stuart and the
Good Hope, but he had never mentioned that Bert was his nephew.
There was no specific reason for him to tell her that, she supposed, but there was no reason for him not to either. How much
else had he held back, and why?

"I was just thinking about the *Virginia II*," she said.

He nodded, rocking slowly back and forth. "A great old boat.
Those were grand times. Before the—before the accident, I
mean."

Lee chewed and swallowed a sweet, sticky mouthful. "I wonder how it got its name," she said casually.

In mid-rock, with the mug just coming away from his mouth,
he stopped so suddenly that he would have slopped coffee over
the side if it hadn't been half-empty. He recovered quickly, swat-
ting at his forearm, pretending that he'd been bothered by a bug.

So he knew about Ginny too.

"Good question," he said, restarting the chair. "As I recall, it
got named for one of Andy's relatives."

Not a lie, but not exactly the truth either. What else did he know that he was choosing not to tell?

"It was mostly Andy's money that bought it, so we figured he ought to get to pick the name, why not?" He stood up, anxious to leave now. "Well, gotta get going. Have a good day, Lee."

She watched him hurry away, leaving the chair rocking. What did she suspect him of, anyway? Murder? No, or at least she didn't think so, but who knew for sure? Besides, she already had her prime suspect; that was what she was going into town to talk to the police about.

With that she wiped her sticky fingers, got up, carried her dishes through the lobby—Benny, behind his desk, pointedly had his nose buried in his accounts—put them on a kitchen cart near the dining room door, and strode out onto Spring Street. The police station was on the far side of town, almost to New Harbor, a mile or more from the inn, but she decided to walk, to give herself time to think things through one more time before talking to Tolliver and perhaps making a fool of herself.

But no, the more she thought about it, the more sense it made. So many things pointed to Darlene, including an additional factor she hadn't thought about before. That thug had been there *waiting* for Darlene in the thick, tall rough beside the fourth fairway. He had parked his truck on the shoulder of the road to wait for her. Well, how had he known to pick that particular spot?

There was only one answer and that was that he knew she would be there. Darlene had hit her ball there on purpose because she knew *he* would be there. She was a good enough player to do it and make it look accidental, and besides, she had a natural hook that sent most of her drives to the left, so there was nothing unusual about it. In this case, however, it had hit a tree and bounced back thirty or forty yards. But Darlene hadn't gone to where the ball had ended up, she'd gone to where it had entered the woods—because she knew fatso would be there waiting. Lee had thought it was because she hadn't seen her ball strike the tree, but why wouldn't she have? Lee had seen it. Ginny had seen it. Even Frank would have seen it if he hadn't been so busy with his "Elbows in . . . check" mantra. So why hadn't Darlene?

"Lee! Wait up!"

The commanding voice brought her up short. She turned. Water Street was full of people, but there was no one she knew.

"I'm over here."

Lee looked to her left, at the entrance porch of the stately old National Hotel, and came near swallowing her tongue when she saw the familiar figure marching down the front steps toward her. Good gosh, speak of the devil.

"What are you doing here in town?" Darlene Chappell asked, or rather demanded. She was in full Grand Czarina mode, regal and elegant in a robin's-egg-blue cashmere blazer, a mannish, tailored, plaid shirt, and dark blue slacks. Her hair, except for a few artfully disarranged strands, was tied back in a small twist. Her face was scrupulously made up, more than ever like a porcelain mask.

Oh, nothing much, Lee thought, while she groped for something to say, *just heading in to tell the chief of police I think you murdered your husband.*

"Well . . . there's no golf this morning, and I . . . but what are *you* doing here, Darlene? I thought you were in Boston."

"No, I'm here," Darlene said in that curt way of hers. "And I'm glad I ran into you."

Darlene had a way of turning whatever she said into a challenge, a command, or a put-down. Lee waited to see which it would be this time. She couldn't think of any reason Darlene would be glad to see her, and she sure wasn't glad to have run into Darlene.

It was a command. "I want you to come with me," Darlene said. "I'm on my way to the police station."

"You are? I was just—"

"Whatever it is can wait; this is more important. I'm afraid I've gotten you pretty deeply involved too, so I suppose you have a right to be there. And I know the police will want to hear what you have to say about it too."

Did that mean what Lee thought it did? She studied Darlene for a long moment. "You're going to confess, aren't you?"

Darlene didn't fluster easily, you had to give her that. "Yes, that's right," she said.

Chapter 17

"Feature that," said Chief Tolliver.

Even for him this was a spectacular show of unflappability. Darlene had just walked into his office with Lee in tow, had plopped herself into a chair, and had bluntly told him that she engineered her own kidnapping to get money from a harshly tight-fisted Stuart to pay off certain debts that she had, that she had hired a small-time gangster to play out the carefully staged abduction scene with her, and that she herself had typed the ransom note and deposited it in the Mooncussers mailbox.

"We'd have damn well gotten away with it too, if she"—a scalding look ·was flung at Lee—"hadn't come bumbling by to stick her nose into it."

Lee, who had been sitting quietly and minding her own business, flared up. "Bumbling in! That stupid stunt cost me my new wedge. As far as I'm concerned, you owe me a hundred and fifty dollars, lady!"

Tolliver smiled at Lee. "In any case, you surely were right there in the thick of it, Miss Ofsted. How does what you've been hearing square with the way you saw things?"

The chief's lazy affability calmed her down. "Very well, Chief Tolliver. As a matter of fact I was on my way—" She bit her tongue. She didn't see much benefit in telling him that she had solved his case for him before he had, or rather before Darlene had. "It fits perfectly."

Tolliver turned back to Darlene, who seemed to have finished her prepared speech and was sitting there with her chin tilted up and a queenly, you-may-now-ask-me-whatever-you-wish look on her face.

"And what were these certain debts?" he asked.

"They're not pertinent. They're personal and long-standing."

And humongous, Lee thought. Well over half a million dollars. Not your everyday boutique bills, even if you were Darlene. She waited with interest and a certain amount of pleasant anticipation for Tolliver to bat aside her patronizing response and follow up.

He didn't. "I see," he said quietly, and began to fill his pipe.

Lee's doubts about him resurfaced. He was a nice enough guy, but if you asked her he seemed a little low on energy to be much of a cop. He didn't pursue questions, he didn't get out in the field, he didn't seem to pay a lot of attention to what you told him; he just sat around in his office waiting for things to come to him. Was that a way to run a police department?

On the other hand, she had to admit that it seemed to be working for him well enough so far.

He got his pipe and took a lengthy pull, careful to expel the smoke in a direction away from them. "I'll need to know the name of the man you hired."

"Felix Grumbo," Darlene said promptly. "We got his name from a rather shady private detective that a cousin of mine once used. That's G-R-U-M-B-O. He lives in Providence somewhere, I don't know the address. His number is 555-0599."

"Mm," said Tolliver. His pipe had quickly gone out, and he concentrated on getting it relit, using two matches before he got it going to his satisfaction. He hadn't bothered to write down what she'd told him. "Mrs. Chappell, I wonder if you'd like to tell me what it is that makes you come in and tell me this now."

"Very well," Darlene said, as if acceding to the wish of a courtier to approach to kiss her hand. "Captain——"

"Chief," said Tolliver.

"Chief Tolliver," Darlene said, "I want the person responsible for my husband's murder caught. And I've come to the conclusion that my—my little hoax on the golf course the other day might interfere with that. That is, it would be only natural for you to think the two events were related."

"And they're not?" Tolliver asked mildly, his head bent while he used a straightened paper clip to dig around in that damn pipe of his.

"Certainly not! I did *not* kill my own husband!" A purplish flush bloomed suddenly on Darlene's cheeks. She sat stiffly forward, her hands on the desk. "You have to believe that."

From under his eyebrows Tolliver glanced at Lee as if to say: "What do you think? Do *you* believe it?"

Did she? She wasn't sure. With a few words Darlene had turned everything topsy-turvy. Everything Lee and Peg and Graham had talked about was based on the premise that Stuart had been killed because he knew who the kidnapper was, or at least that there had to be some connection to the attempt. And now Darlene was saying that it wasn't so, that the two incidents had nothing to do with one another.

"It's true, damn you!" Darlene snapped when the chief didn't say anything.

Lee realized with some surprise that she didn't want to believe her. In the first place, it was just too incredible that the one could have nothing at all to do with the other, that it was just a coincidence that two such bizarre things had happened within two days of each other. And in the second place—and this is what came as a surprise, and not a very agreeable one—Lee suddenly understood that she *wanted* Darlene to be guilty, that she was looking forward to Darlene's being guilty. It made sense for Darlene to be guilty. If anybody had to have been responsible for Stuart's murder, and of course somebody did, then the Grand Czarina was head and shoulders out in front of anybody else as her favorite candidate.

And yet there was something utterly believable about her at this moment, about the darkening flush that had now spread to her throat, about the urgent, even frightened tremor in her voice despite the arrogance of that "damn you." And coincidences *did* happen.

"Would I have come here and admitted the kidnapping plot if I'd killed him?" Darlene asked Tolliver. "I'd have been out of my mind to do that, can't you see that?"

Yes, Lee did see that. Reluctantly she came around a little more yet. It began to look as if they were going to need a new prime suspect.

"I still don't know why you did come here," Tolliver said.

"I just told you. Because I didn't want you and your people wasting their time investigating a stupid, harmless little charade—"

Lee's eyebrows went up. Harmless? What about that wedge?

"—while a *murderer*, my husband's murderer, for God's sake!—gets further and further away from being caught."

"I see," said Tolliver. He was wreathed in fragrant, blue-gray smoke now. Above him it rose to the ceiling and pancaked into thin, hazy sheets against the fluorescent light fixture in the ceiling. "Who was involved in the kidnapping with you, Mrs. Chappell?"

"I told you that all of two minutes ago. Do you think it might help if you wrote it down?" The arrogant snap was back in her voice. She was sounding like the old Darlene again. "Felix Grumbo," she said, emphasizing each syllable. "G-R-U-M—"

"No, I mean who else?"

She blinked. "I have no idea what you mean."

"What you said to me two minutes ago," the chief said, then paused to pluck a shred of tobacco from his tongue, examine it with interest, and reinsert the pipe into his mouth, "was, 'We got his name from a rather shady private detective that a cousin of mine once used.' Now, what I'm asking you, y'see, is: who's 'we'?"

Now it was Lee who blinked. What do you know about that, Tolliver was awake after all. Wide awake too. She had heard that "we" as well as he had, but it had gone right by her. And here he was, not only remembering but quoting the whole sentence verbatim. No wonder the guy didn't take notes; he didn't have to.

"It was a figure of speech," Darlene said with an elaborately impatient sigh.

Tolliver peered at her through another leisurely outpouring of smoke. "I don't think so," he said.

Lee continued to be impressed. Somehow, just sitting there puffing on his pipe and speaking quietly, he had shifted the balance of power in the little office. He was suddenly in charge. Darlene was on the defensive and it was obvious that they both knew it.

"You can think what you like," she began tartly, then decided to give it up. "All right, you're right. There was a—a friend—"

"Another man," Tolliver said.

Darlene's thin mouth tightened. A shadow of the flush returned. "Yes, a man, a lover if that's what you want to know, but it's nobody here on the island, nobody you know. Even Stuart was completely unaware of his existence. He lives in Florida, he has a life of his own, far away from this mess, and I'm not going to involve him in it."

Tolliver looked at Lee. "Any ideas, Miss Ofsted?"

Lee shook her head.

"I *told* you," Darlene said to Tolliver, "I don't want him involved."

"Well, we'll see," Tolliver said.

"We will *not* see."

She glared at Tolliver until he dropped his eyes, but at this point, Lee was betting on him being the one to get his way in the end.

"This debt you mentioned before," Tolliver said calmly. "That's not quite what it was, is it? You wanted the money from your husband so that you and your . . . friend could go off together and make a new life. Isn't that right?"

Darlene looked stonily at him, refusing to answer, her mouth as flat and hard as a vise.

Son of a gun, Lee thought, this rural police chief was really something. He'd hit the nail right on the head, it was written all over her face. Only why the weird ransom amount? What was that all about?

"All right then, Mrs. Chappell," Tolliver said without offense, "I wonder if you could help me out on an entirely different subject."

"Certainly," Darlene said, relaxing into something like graciousness. "What would you like to know?"

"It's about your husband's will. His lawyer isn't making it real easy for us to have a look at it. Now, we're gonna get it eventually, that goes without saying, but I wonder if you could fill me in on a couple of points."

"If I can," Darlene said. "All I know are the broad outlines. Stuart wasn't a forthright man about such matters, and I won't be meeting with Mr. Glenn to hear the specifics until Monday. What points did you have in mind?"

"Well, basically, who the main beneficiaries are."

Lee shifted in her chair to make herself a little more inconspicuous. The conversation has strayed pretty far away from the faked kidnapping and she knew she didn't have any business being there. But both Darlene and Tolliver seemed to have forgotten about her, and as long as they didn't mind, she wasn't about to leave. She was all ears. And, after all, she'd been invited.

"That's easy enough," Darlene said. "Once various specific bequests have been made to a number of individual and institutional beneficiaries, the residuary estate, including the homes in Boston and St. Thomas, will go to me. I don't know the exact amount."

"Must be a tidy sum, though," Tolliver observed. His pipe had gone out again. He laid it in an ashtray.

"I won't be going hungry, if that's what you mean," Darlene said with a rare smile, "but of course the bulk of Stuart's wealth is in SRS, not in his personal assets, and the company is going, lock, stock, and barrel"—she paused, eyes perfectly expressionless—"to Malcolm."

Malcolm! Lee very nearly blurted.

"Malcolm Labrecque," the impassive Tolliver said, nodding.

"Yes. You're aware, of course, that Malcolm is Stuart's stepson."

This time Lee couldn't help it. "His *stepson!*" she yelped, practically jumping out of her chair. It was amazing; the whole company was this incredible tangle of relationships. Malcolm was

Stuart's stepson, Ginny was Andy's daughter, Bert was Benny's nephew . . .

The others paid no attention to the outburst. "His first wife's son," Tolliver said thoughtfully. "I understand your husband raised the boy."

"Yes. Stuart was never a man to shirk his obligations."

"Do the others know about Malcolm?"

"I'm sure they don't. Stuart preferred to keep it to himself."

"So Malcolm gets the company on Stuart's death." Tolliver seemed to roll the words around his mouth like a cow working on its cud. "That's interesting."

"Yes, isn't it? And now, Chief Tolliver, I think I've said all I wanted to say." Darlene rose, trim and authoritative in her blue blazer. "I think you know where you can reach me." She glanced at Lee as one might glance at a child or a pet, as if to say: *Come, Lee.* Lee half expected her to snap her fingers.

Lee stayed put—it was up to Tolliver, not Darlene, to dismiss her, and the chief hadn't told her to leave. His cracked leather chair creaked as he leaned back to look up at Darlene. "Sit down, Mrs. Chappell, we're not through. But I think maybe you ought to be running along, Miss Ofsted."

That was that, then. Time to go. Lee got up. Darlene, who had remained standing, said, "But I *am* through. I came here on my own volition, and you have no right to hold me."

"And why would that be?" Tolliver asked.

Darlene smiled again. Amazing; twice inside of an hour. "I assure you, I've discussed this thoroughly with my lawyer in Boston. What would you hold me for? I've committed no crime."

"How's that again?"

"The kidnapping failed. It never happened." She spread her hands palms-up. "There *was* no crime."

Tolliver looked at her with a kind of amused tolerance.

"Lady, if I was you, I'd find another lawyer. And for starters, you better tell him to read up on extortion."

Darlene faltered. "On . . . on . . ."

"Extortion," Tolliver said, standing, then added mildly: "E-X-T-O-R-T-I-O-N." He waited for Darlene to reply, but when she didn't he went on. "Ma'am, I don't know whether you killed your husband or not, maybe yes, maybe no, but I do know that you tried to extort six hundred and fifty thousand dollars from him, because you just told me so. And that, ma'am, is a crime." He turned to Lee, who'd been too engrossed to move. "Bye-bye," he said, gesturing her toward the door with a waggle of his fingers. "I'll be in touch."

"I want to talk to my lawyer," a wooden Darlene said.

As she closed the door behind her, the last words Lee heard were the chief's.

"You mean your own Boston lawyer, or did you want me to find a good one here on the island?"

Chapter 18

Lee's mind was buzzing with questions as she stepped out of the police station and began walking back toward downtown. If Darlene hadn't killed her husband, then who had? And what did this latest surprise in the SRS family saga say about Malcolm? Did it make him a more likely candidate? On the one hand, sure: he'd certainly gained the most from Stuart's death. On the other, not so sure: would he have committed murder to get something that would eventually have come to him anyway? Especially when it was his own father that had to be done away with? Could he—could any sane human being—really drive a spike into the throat of the dead or unconscious man who'd raised him? It was too horrible to think about.

But on the other hand—if there was still another hand—Malcolm was the son of Stuart's long-ago first wife. Was there really much of a bond? From Stuart to Malcolm, obviously yes; from Malcolm to Stuart, maybe not. How had Malcolm felt as a child when Stuart had gone and left him and his mother? Had he been bearing a grudge ever since, just biding his time?

Whatever the case, it was clear now why Malcolm had so confidently slipped into what Peg had called his Simon Legree mode, except that his Royal Majesty mode was more like it; Malcolm wasn't just the new veep, he was the owner, the president, the heir, the boss's son, and the new boss, all rolled into one.

And if recent experience was any guide, he had no doubt decreed a working lunch for his hapless subjects, and Peg as well, which meant they'd be munching cold cuts over their strategic parameters in the Dory Room about now. That being the case, Lee stopped in at the Harborside Inn for a hamburger, then hurried up the hill to the Mooncussers in hopes of catching Peg after lunch. Surely even Malcolm would allow a fifteen- or twenty-minute after-lunch breather before getting their noses back to the grindstone, and Lee could hardly wait to talk to Peg; they hadn't compared notes since yesterday, over Chinese chicken and snow peas, and a lot had come to light since then. Or maybe "light" was the wrong word. The more facts that came out, the murkier things seemed to get.

But none of them were around. Benny, who had lost all inclination to chat with her since she'd brought up the subject of the *Virginia II,* merely handed her a telephone message and an envelope from a niche in the Chinese whatnot, then buried his nose back in whatever he was working on or pretending to work on at his desk. It seemed obvious that he was protecting Ginny by trying to keep his prior knowledge to himself, much as he had been protecting Bert by not revealing the family connection there. What was less obvious was whether he *knew* that either or both of them were involved in recent events, or was simply afraid that they *might* be.

All things considered, Lee thought the latter was more likely.

The telephone message was from Graham. He had indeed finished up early and would be arriving at the Block Island airport at three-thirty. Could she meet him?

Could she! Smiling happily, she turned to the envelope. Inside was a note from Peg, scrawled on both sides of the sheet.

1 P.M.

Lee:

   Simon L. has decided in his wisdom that the SRS people need some time to work things through by themselves with no pushy consultant hanging around.

   Needless to say, I did not argue the point.

   So now I'm like you, a lady of leisure—till dinner, anyway—and I've gone out to the range for a last look at Jackie's toys to see what I want to buy myself for a birthday present. Why don't you come on out and join me? You can sell it to me and earn a 20% commission!

   And then maybe we could actually do a round of golf for the fun of it? When was the last time you did that? For the fun of it, I mean?

   AND WAIT'LL YOU HEAR WHAT I HAVE TO TELL YOU!! I'm brilliant! (Wear old socks, because this is going to blow them off!)

Peg

Lee glanced at her watch. One-thirty-five. No time for golf before she went to the airport, but plenty of time to swing by the course for a chat. Naturally enough, Peg's note had piqued her interest, but she was looking forward even more to the pleasure of springing her own astonishing news on her old pal. Peg had better make sure her own socks were securely hitched up.

*   *   *

"Good gosh, what *is* that?"

"Don't make me laugh," said Peg, laughing. "This band from my belt to my wrist is supposed to make sure my left arm and shoulder come around on the hip turn, and this band around my waist that's attached to this post here is supposed to heighten the sense of coiling on the backswing, and this other thingy from my left shoulder to my side is supposed to—well, I forget what it's supposed to do, but if it pops apart during the backswing it's bad news. And this little dealie over here—"

"Peg, you're not actually going to try to swing a golf club while you're in that contraption? It looks like it came out of Dracula's dungeon."

"Well, I've been thinking about it, but with all these damn bands and everything, I can't figure out how to get started."

"Don't. You'll break something. And besides I want to hear what you have to tell me."

Peg's eyes lit up. She tossed her club into a rack. "Wait'll you hear. Help me get out of this first, will you?"

But she was too impatient to wait, and she got started talking while the two of them were undoing snaps and ripping apart Velcro tabs. "Listen to this. I was playing around on the computer with Consumer Price Index figures to determine the relative values of—"

"Hold it, I'm lost already."

"All right, sorry. I'll cut to the good stuff. Do you happen to remember how much money Stuart made in 1971 on the *Good Hope*?"

"Um, two hundred thousand—no, two hundred and eight thousand dollars."

"Correct. Now: do you recall the amount of the ransom the other day?"

"Six hundred and fifty-nine thousand?"

"Six hundred and fifty thousand, nine hundred and ninety-three. Very good. Final question: would you care to take an educated guess as to how much six hundred and fifty thousand, nine hundred and ninety-three dollars in today's money was worth in 1971?"

Lee sighed. "Peg, how about just . . ." She ground to a halt. "You're going to tell me it would have been worth two hundred and eight thousand dollars, aren't you? Which would mean," she went on, almost as excited as Peg, "that the amount of the ransom was based—"

"No," Peg said, laughing, "that's not what I'm going to tell you, but you're warm. I'm going to tell you that six hundred and fifty thousand, nine hundred and ninety-three dollars in today's money would have been worth—are you ready for this?—one hundred and seventy-three thousand dollars in 1971."

Lee frowned. "So what the heck does a hundred and—"

"Do you remember telling me that after the *Good Hope* affair Stuart gave thirty thousand dollars of his profits to Andy Gottlieb's family—to Ginny and her mother?"

Lee nodded.

"And do you remember my telling you that Frank got five thousand?"

"Yes," Lee said between clenched teeth, "and although this is all terrifically suspenseful, it would be nice if you got to the—"

"Thirty thousand plus five thousand is thirty-five thousand," said Peg, "and if you subtract thirty-five thousand from two hundred and eight thousand you get . . . would you care to hazard a guess?"

"One hundred and seventy-three thousand!" Lee clapped her hands together. "Peg, you *are* brilliant!"

"Tut," said Peg. "Anyone with a minimal knowledge of the application of price-and-demand elasticity to microeconomic theory could have done the same." She unhooked a final clasp on the band around her hips, detaching herself from the last of the three posts she'd been hooked up to. "Free at last! Come on, let's go over to the shed and see if there's something cold to drink."

"I have some interesting news too," Lee said as they walked to the shed.

But Peg was still absorbed in her own discoveries. "You do see what this means, don't you? The ransom was based precisely on Stuart's profits from the *Good Hope*—precisely and very fairly, even allowing for the rate of inflation right down to the nearest dollar. *Compulsively* precisely, you might say." She darted an inquisitive look at Lee. "Does that suggest anybody to you?"

"Suggest anybody? As the kidnapper, is that what you're asking?"

"Of course that's what I'm asking. The kidnapper *and* the murderer. You bet that's what I'm asking."

"Ah. Well, as a matter of fact, the kidnapper—"

"And the answer is *Malcolm.* It has to be, don't you agree? Who else would be obsessive enough to dream up something like that?"

"Oh, Malcolm," Lee said. "Well, Malcolm, as it turns out, is—"

But once Peg had hold of something, getting her attention wasn't that easy. "But that still leaves us with a lot of unanswered questions," she went on. "Why would Malcolm have any kind of grudge against Stuart over the *Good Hope*? He wasn't involved in it, at least as far as we know, and besides, he would have been—what, fifteen years old? And as for kidnapping Darlene, I just can't—"

Abruptly Lee stamped her foot. "*Peg!* Will you let me say something? Please?"

Peg looked blandly at her. "You wanted to say something?"

"I want to say three things. Will you let me get them all out?"

"Well, of course I will." She peered into the ice chest in the shed. "Rats, no ice. Want a warm 7 Up?"

"No, thanks. First, Malcolm Labrecque is Stuart's stepson by his first marriage."

"Stuart's stepson! How in the world—"

"Peg, you promised."

"Sorry."

"Second, there never really was a kidnapping attempt. It was a hoax. And—"

"A hoax! You're—oops, sorry, sorry."

"And third, the person behind it was Darlene herself."

"Darlene! Lee, how did you come up with all this?"

"I spent the morning at the police station. I had a front-row seat for a session between Darlene and Tolliver."

"But I thought Darlene was back in—hey, how did you get to sit in on—Lee, dammit, why didn't you tell me all this before?"

Lee just looked at her and laughed.

"Whew," Peg said, drooping, "this is almost too much to process. I think my hard disk just crashed. Let's go think awhile."

She popped the top of a warm can of 7 Up and the two of them drifted from the shed to sit side by side in a golf cart overlooking the driving range, their feet propped on the control panel. It was strange to see the place so deserted; all spruced up for the about-to-begin season, but with no one at the tees, no one on the practice green, no one at the crazy lineup of Stroke-Cutters.

Peg surfaced first. "Look, if what you just said about Darlene is true, then Darlene must have killed Stuart too, right? I mean, she must have. Because it only stands to reason. The kidnapping got bollixed up, Stuart found out Darlene was behind it, and D—"

Lee shook her head. "I don't know. That's the way it looked

to me last night, but she did come in on her own to confess to the phony kidnap—nobody made her do it—and she swears she doesn't know anything about Stuart's death."

"And you believe her?"

"Well, she was pretty convincing. Apparently she's got a boyfriend tucked away somewhere and the ransom was their way of getting a little nest egg for themselves."

"Right, and when it didn't work out as planned, she killed him so she could use her *inheritance* as the nest egg. Plan B. The weird ransom amount and the spike were just window dressing. Smoke and mirrors."

Lee nodded. "You could be right."

"Company," Peg said, looking toward one of the inn's rental cars winding up the drive toward the range. "That's Jackie, isn't it?"

It was. He parked in the nearby gravel lot and climbed out. "Say," he said, studying Lee, "don't I know you from somewhere? The face looks familiar but I can't quite place . . ."

"Don't rub it in," Lee said. "I already feel guilty enough for not earning my pay." She meant it too. Since Tuesday she had worked exactly one hour—the session on putting—and this was Friday, so if you prorated it, her salary over the last three days came to $3,000 an hour. And it had been a pretty lackluster hour at that.

"I'm glad to hear it," Jackie told her, "because I was about to ask you to give me a hand packing up the Stroke-Cutters."

"I'd love to," Lee said, getting out of the cart.

"I'll help too," Peg said.

"All offers cheerfully accepted. So tell me, what's new? I've been in Southampton making hay since yesterday. No point in just sitting around if there's nothing doing. Idle hands and all that. So what's the latest? Any more excitement? Anybody else get kidnapped? Anyone get arrested? I just drove in from the air-port, I haven't even stopped at the inn."

"The latest," said Peg, "is that there never was a kidnapping. Darlene engineered it herself."

Jackie started to laugh, then stared at her. "Say *what?*"

Peg explained, happily feasting on Jackie's lively astonishment. He made her go over the details twice and even then had a hard time taking it in.

"I can't believe it!" he cried. "It's too wild! She actually came in from Boston and *confessed*? Did they arrest her?"

Peg blinked and looked at Lee. "Did they? I was so excited I forgot to ask you."

"I don't know myself," Lee told them. "She sure wasn't ex-pecting to be held, that was clear, but when I left them Chief Tolliver had a pretty steely glint in his eye, so maybe he did it." She pointed at the equipment. "Jackie, if I'm going to help, we'd better get started. I have to be at the airport in an hour to pick up Graham."

"Right, right," said Jackie reluctantly. "Time's awasting, I sup-pose. I have to air-express it all off the island no later than to-morrow morning if I want to have them up and ready in Southampton on Tuesday."

"You're doing another course at Southampton?" Lee asked.

"I do an annual refresher at Dune Point, and I can hardly wait. I love that course, and I *love* Southampton, it's wonderful! I'd ask you to help again, but this one I do by myself."

He launched into a foot-stamping little Mexican hat dance, complete with lyrics. "*La cucaracha, la cucaracha,* Southampton here I come."

"That's a nice course, Dune Point," Lee said.

"Yes, and there's a better grade of clientele there. Nobody ever seems to get murdered, at least not at my school."

"Amen to that," Peg said.

"And it's always great to visit my plaque in the clubhouse. It reminds me that I qualify as a certified has-been, not just another never-was."

"You have a plaque at the Dune Point clubhouse?" Peg asked. "What's that all about?"

"I thought you'd never ask. Okay, get ready for a thrill." He drew himself up to his full five-nine and thumped on his chest, bringing forth a mock cough. "You happen to be looking at Dune Point's low-score record-holder in tournament play—a sixty-two, shot one fine day in April of 1991."

"Wow," said Lee, "I've played that course. That's a heck of a score."

"And in heavy-duty competition, no less. I suppose you ladies are too young to remember, but they used to hold the Wheatix Open there, and I scored that sixty-two on the first day of play. I was in first place after one round, in sixteenth place after two, in forty-fourth after three, and—well, never mind where I was at the end." He sighed. "That's what happens when you're playing with the big boys, but it was marvelous while it lasted. That was my last year on the tour, you know. I knew I wasn't ever going to have a better day than that, so I figured I might as well quit. Good thing I did too." He wiped imaginary sweat from his forehead. "Just think, if I hadn't, the world might never have had the Jackie Piper Stroke-Cutter method, and then where would we all be?"

"We'd all have more money to spend on other things, that's where," Peg said. "Say, Jackie, if I remember right, Darlene was at the Wheatix in '91. Did you happen to run into her?"

"Darlene? You mean our Darlene? No, I didn't know she was that much of a golf fan."

"Oh, sure, and she used to be a golf model, and the thing is, there's this story going around about her . . ."

"Oh, good. A juicy one, I hope. Well, come on, come on, don't hold back, I'm all ears. Or can you tell it in mixed company?"

Something prickled at the back of Lee's neck. The words, the sprightly tone, the bright peal of little-boy laughter were vintage Jackie, but somehow it all fell flat, missed the mark. The briefest of tics flickered below his right eye until he stiffened his cheek and brought it under control. The realization flowed over her like a great, suffocating wave. Oh my God, Lee thought, it's *you!* You're the "other man," you're the "big-name pro" from the Wheatix Open, you're Darlene's lover! She lied to Tolliver— you're not in Florida, you're right *here* . . . Lee looked down, up, sideways, any way at all to keep herself from staring at him.

But of course Peg was barreling blithely along. "Unfortunately I don't have all the details. I was hoping you did. Are you sure you never heard about it? Maybe you just don't remember her name because you didn't know her then, but everybody says she and one of the pros . . ."

Peg, shut up! Lee sent vibes, made faces, transferred thoughts, did everything she could short of speech to get her friend to be quiet, and something must have gotten through because in the middle of her sentence Peg stammered and changed direction ". . . Well, what difference does it make what everybody says, it's probably all just a lot of catty gossip anyway."

"Probably, but I'm the last one to say anything against catty gossip," Jackie said. "Come on, don't leave me hanging."

"Oh, it's . . . it's not really worth—"

"If we're really going to get anything done today," Lee put in, "I think we'd better get going, don't you?" She started walking them toward the equipment.

"Spoilsport," Jackie said, "but I suppose you're right. May as well start with the biggie, the Triple-P; that's the bulkiest job." He pointed at the one Personal Plane Partner that was still standing, Frank Wishniak having effectively demolished the other three with his sensational, dominoeslike tumble.

"Lee, if you and Peg will . . . oh, damn, we'll need an Allen wrench, won't we? I've got one in my toolbox in the clubhouse. Hold the fort, back in a sec." He trotted off toward the gray-shingled shack that served as the clubhouse.

Lee and Peg stared at each other. "Holy cow," Peg whispered, "you don't really think . . ."

"I sure do! It has to be him, Peg! He was the one she had the affair with in '91—didn't you see his face when you brought it up? He almost came apart. And he's still her lover! He was in with her on the kidnapping—and he was in with her on the murder. Everything hangs together now. Darlene was lying when she said he was somebody we didn't know, and she was lying when she said she had nothing to do with killing Stuart."

"But then why would she be crazy enough to confess to the kidnapping hoax? Why didn't she just stay back in Boston where she was safely out of it?"

"I don't know."

"And why in the world would she come in and confess without telling Jackie? Because unless he's an even better actor than I thought, that news knocked him for a loop."

"I don't know that either, but they're in it together, all right. Look, am I wrong, or didn't you tell me that the golf package with Jackie was Darlene's idea?"

"That's true, it was." Peg chewed on her lip. She was starting to come around.

"And that you had no idea why she came up with it?"

"Well, yes, I guess I did say that."

"Well, now you know. It was all carefully worked out ahead of time, Peg. Maybe not killing Stuart, but certainly the phony kidnapping."

Peg glanced anxiously toward the clubhouse. No sign of Jackie yet. "You don't think he knows we're on to him?"

"I don't think so, but I suggest we don't wait around to find out. Let's—yikes, here he comes."

Peg laid her hand on Lee's forearm. "Just be calm," she whispered.

"I *am* calm. I'm just scared stiff, that's all. What if he—"

"Just play it straight, as if nothing's happened. We'll help him with the equipment for a few minutes, then leave. Just be natural, be cheerful . . . Well, *hel*-lo, Jackie!" she piped, very natural, very cheerful (and only about two octaves above normal). "Got the wrench?"

"Right here," he said—a little brightly, Lee thought, feeling the faint beginnings of a sinking sensation around her heart. He placed a dented red toolbox on the ground next to the Personal Plane Partner, squatted to undo the clasp, reached in, and stood up, his right hand extended.

Lee's heart promptly dropped the rest of the way, clunking to a stop somewhere around her knees. In Jackie's hand, clutched much too convulsively for her peace of mind, was a black, blunt, dully gleaming, snub-nosed revolver, not unlike the ugly Detective Special that Graham used to carry in a holster under his arm.

Peg did what Lee couldn't and responded with style. "Excuse me, Jackie, but would you mind pointing that Allen wrench somewhere else?"

But for once Jackie's sense of humor had deserted him. "Shut up!"

They waited for him to say more but he just stared at them,

his mouth working. He looked dogged and frightened at the same time, as if he couldn't decide whether to shoot them on the spot and run for it or just to fling the gun down, burst into tears, and throw himself on their mercy.

Peg shot a quick glance at Lee: *We'd better do something.*

Lee threw one back: *You bet, but what?*

Jackie stood about six feet from them, at the head of the Personal Plane Partner, apparently pondering their fate, the gun pointed vaguely in their direction, sometimes wavering one way, sometimes the other, sometimes up, sometimes down. Lee had read somewhere, or maybe Graham had told her, that a revolver like that didn't need a safety because it took fourteen or fifteen pounds of pressure to pull the trigger. She hoped that was right; Jackie's hand, his whole right arm, was shaking.

"Look, I don't know what this is all about," Peg said at last, "but if it's supposed to be a joke—"

"What did I just tell you? Didn't I tell you to shut up? I have to *think*." Distractedly, almost comically, like a silent-movie actor portraying consternation, he kneaded his forehead, massaged the area around his mouth, dug his fingers through his springy hair, absently reached out to clasp one of the seven-foot-long metal legs that supported the higher end of the Plexiglas sheet.

Lee and Peg exchanged another furtive glance, moving only their eyes. The collapsible metal pole he was holding on to was attached to a corner of the Plexiglass at an angle, splayed out toward the front and side to provide stability. The bottom of it was no more than two feet from Lee's left foot.

She held her breath and stepped timidly, unthreateningly toward him. "Jackie—"

"Stay right there!"

She did. But she had managed a single, all-important step. The rubber-tipped foot of the pole that supported the heavy sheet of plastic was about fifteen inches from her toes. Within reach.

Jackie didn't notice. He was still holding on to the pole at shoulder height, leaning perhaps a quarter of his weight on it. "You people have really screwed things up, you know that?" He was still nervous but making an effort at getting back his old cockiness. He moved his gun hand up to rub the area under his eyes with the back of his hand, leaned a shade more heavily on the pole, opened his mouth to speak—

And went down, flat on his back in the grass, as Lee kicked the pole out from under the Plexiglas and from under Jackie, and the whole contraption, Jackie included, came down in a near repeat of the episode with Frank the day before.

But this time nobody was laughing. Jackie cursed sharply and grabbed for a better hold on the revolver, which had been jarred from his grasp but not out of his hand. Meanwhile, Peg and Lee darted toward the edge of the cliff some thirty feet away, where a steep, rocky path zigzagged down to the beach, but Lee managed only one step before getting her feet tangled in the spidery legs of the upturned Plane Partner and pitching helplessly onto the grass a few feet from Jackie.

He was quick; the gun was focused on her before she'd stopped sprawling. "Run, Peg!" she shouted, seeing out of the corner of her eye that her friend, hearing her fall, had stopped near the edge of the cliff and was peering irresolutely back.

"Stop! Stop!" Jackie screamed, swinging the gun jerkily around to aim it more or less at Peg, who paused only a fraction of a second before deciding whose advice to follow. With two more running steps she was at the top of the path and starting down.

Jackie yelled again. "Stop!" When she didn't, he hurriedly aimed at her crouched, darting form and pulled the trigger. His hand was only a couple of yards from Lee's ear and she winced automatically, but the gun's report in the open air was strangely puny, a dull, flat, unauthoritative *crack*. The recoil that jerked his arm back was impressive enough, however, and Peg again halted momentarily to stare at him in indignant amazement, as if she couldn't believe he was actually being rude enough to fire a gun at her, then disappeared over the rim, obviously unhurt.

Jackie was on his feet in a flash, but once up he faced a dilemma. Lee, anticipating that he would chase after Peg, had instinctively gathered her legs under her and pushed herself up onto her fingertips like a runner, tensing her muscles in preparation for a dash in the opposite direction the instant she had a chance. But when he looked at her she froze; he might not be able to shoot straight, but from five feet away he could hardly miss. He looked wildly at her. He looked wildly over his shoulder, toward where Peg had disappeared. As far as Lee could see, he had an impossible choice: he could chase after Peg, in which case Lee would get away, or he could hold on to Lee, in which case Peg would get away.

Of course there was a third possibility too—he could shoot Lee first, thereby removing that danger to himself, and *then* take off after Peg—but Lee put that one out of her mind, hoping it wouldn't occur to him. Still in her kneeling position, she forced herself to relax her bowstring-taut thighs and calves and held up both hands palms-out, trying to calm him down, or at least not to make him any more agitated than he already was.

He came to his decision. "All right, get up, get up," he told her, motioning with the revolver.

She rose, breathing a small sigh of relief. He could have shot her just as well crouching down as standing up, so apparently he didn't intend killing her, at least for the moment. Keeping his eyes on her and the gun trained in her direction, he knelt to open the toolbox again, groping around in it and coming out this time with a pair of handcuffs.

Lee stifled what must have been a semihysterical giggle. Gun, handcuffs . . . what else did he keep in that thing? Was there truly an Allen wrench somewhere in there, or was it just his own little fun-and-games collection that he carried around with him from place to place?

"Here," he said, handing the cuffs to her. "Snap one on."

She took them. She had seen handcuffs before, in a little leather belt pouch that Graham sometimes used to wear, but she'd never handled them. "I don't know how."

He scowled at her. "Don't fool around. Just snap it closed."

She did, accidentally squeezing it a notch too far. "Ow, I made it too tight."

"Turn around and put your hands behind you."

"I'm telling you, it's hurting my—"

"Lee, don't mess with me, dammit!" he shrieked so shrilly that it made her jump. Whew, he was genuinely ready to come unglued. "Do you think I'm kidding around? Do you think I wouldn't kill you?" He waved the gun, shook it at her, so close to her face she could smell the oil. "Turn *around!*"

She turned. Jackie pulled both hands behind her and quickly snapped the second cuff on her other wrist. When she heard the click and felt the tug on her wrists, something went out of her. Never before in her life had she had her hands tied behind her, even in childhood games, and at the shock of it her spirit seemed to shrivel up inside her. Until that moment, she had been able to pretend that she still had some control over what was happening; not much, but some, or at least the potential for some. But now she was helpless, utterly vulnerable, utterly in his power.

When he lightly pushed her, urging her toward the car, she went meekly, the sickly taste of fear rising in her throat.

He opened the trunk of the hatchback and motioned her to get in. She bent her head to climb in, but with her hands cuffed behind her she found that it wasn't easy.

Jackie pushed her shoulder downward and shoved, so that she rolled in headfirst, over the lip of the rear bumper. She wound up on her side, facing the back, feeling more helpless than ever, like a trussed-up duck. Her knees were sticking out of the space, but she couldn't get enough leverage to pull them back, so Jackie shoved them down and closed the hatch, leaving her in the dark. She felt the car rock as he leaned on the door, making sure that it was locked, then heard him walk over the gravel, open the front door, and slam it shut as he got into the driver's seat.

When he started up the engine there was a loud, gargly rattle under the floorboards directly beneath her left ear and a faint whiff of gasoline, and then the car moved. She had meant to try to form some mental image of the route they took in case it was helpful later, but quickly found that, although she could sense the turns, she couldn't tell if they were to the left or to the right; indeed, half the time she had the feeling they were going backward, not forward, which couldn't be so. She was able to tell when they left the gravel road for the highway, but that was it. The clattering beneath her ear continued. She tried to twist her head away from it but was wedged into her position and could only move a couple of inches. Worn-out muffler, she thought irritably; you'd think a car rental company would take better care of its equipment.

It wasn't completely dark in the trunk. The ill-fitting inside lid in the hatchback allowed some light to get through, and occasional shadows of branches and glancing rays of sunshine flickered and danced around her, further confusing her sense of direction. She was lying on her side in a fetal position, her head bent forward, so that all she could see clearly were the rounded tops of her own knees. Beyond her feet she knew that there were a couple of wire coat hangers, potential weapons—she had noticed them when Jackie shoved her in—but reaching them was impossible. For some minutes she had strained to reach them with her hands and then with her feet, and then by twisting her whole body around to try to get to them with her teeth, but it couldn't be done, there wasn't enough room to move. And even if it could have been done, where was she supposed to hide them? And even if she hid them, what good would they be against a gun? She gave up at last and eased her contorted limbs back into their original position.

Considering that the whole island was only seven miles long, the drive seemed endless, but she was less uncomfortable than she might have expected. The pain of the tight handcuff had diminished to an irritation now, and the sound of the spent muffler had settled into a steady *pik-a-ta-pik-a-ta*, like the beat of racing railroad wheels, and the shifting, wavering forms of the shadows in front of her eyes were irresistibly lulling. Given all this, she found herself in a sleepy, floating reverie, oddly distant in space and time, as if she were in somebody else's dream—Jackie's maybe.

Did he intend to kill her? How could he not? If he let her go, she would be able to identify him, and how could he let that happen? By the same token, what good would killing her do? Peg was certainly on her way to the police right now, so what would be the point of killing Lee?

But if he didn't mean to kill her, why hadn't he just left her at the range and driven off by himself? She represented no additional danger to him, no more than Peg did by herself. Why had he taken her with him? What *was* his plan? Was she going to be a hostage? Interesting questions all.

There were other interesting questions. Why in the world did Jackie keep a pair of handcuffs in his toolbox? The gun she could understand; he had come to the island prepared to commit a crime, and the possible need for a weapon had to be considered. But handcuffs? How could he have foreseen a use for handcuffs? Or could it be that . . .

When the car left the smooth pavement and bounced onto gravel again, she came sharply back to the present. The strange, floating sense of leisure left her. Wherever they were heading, they were close to getting there. Her breath was coming faster now. The car pulled into a covered space—a carport? a garage?—and stopped. The front door opened and the car rocked a little as Jackie got out. Lee lay there, breathing through her mouth, her eyes open very wide. She could hear her breath in her ears, actually feel the thumping of her heart against her breastbone.

The hatchback door opened. Lee couldn't see him clearly because of the sudden glare, but if his tight, breathless voice was any guide, he was as scared as she was, or maybe more so.

"We're here," he said desolately. "Oh, God."

Chapter 19

It was more of a shack than a house; one of the tiny Colonial cottages that dotted the island. Seen from a distance, seen across fields and pastures and stone walls, it must have been picturesque, an old-fashioned charmer. But seen from the inside it was mildewed and decrepit; clean enough but uncared for, with peeling walls, a deep-seated dankness, and a musty, pervasive odor of old wood, old furniture, and old kitchen grease.

They entered the house through the side door. Through the ugly kitchen with its 1950s electric range, 1940s linoleum floor, and 1920s tin sink, past the still uglier bathroom, and then into the main room, a combination parlor-dining area with a table and chairs at one end and a sofa, a sprung armchair, and an old TV set with a bent coat hanger for an antenna at the other. There were a few flyspecked sailing prints on the walls, and some mounted bric-a-brac cabinets with a sad assortment of kitschy mugs and junky porcelain figurines that must once—a long time ago—have meant something to someone. Against the far wall, near the front door, was a large, silver-painted steam radiator.

"Okay, stop, stand still."

She stopped.

Behind her back, Jackie fiddled with the handcuffs. "I'm going to open one of these. Then I want you to go snap it around the radiator. Around the leg, not around the steam pipe."

"Please, could you undo the other one instead?"

"What? Why?"

"It's tight, and it really hurts."

"Oh, for Christ's sake." He'd already had the other one opened, but he grumbled some more and clicked it shut again, then started on the other one, fumbling because he was still holding the gun and also because Lee's wrists were trembling.

She didn't try to control this because she knew that Jackie thought she was shaking from an overwhelming sense of fright and defeat, and that was the way she wanted it. In truth, she *was* frightened, yes, but she was a long way from defeated, and she was trembling more from pent-up tension than from fear. When the clasp around her right wrist sprang open she was going to walk toward the radiator as if following his instructions, then whirl suddenly to her left and catch him backhanded in the face with all her might with the loose, dangling handcuffs. They weren't heavy enough to do him any real damage unless she was lucky enough to catch him across the eyes, but it would be enough to startle him, maybe knock him off his feet. Then she would go for the heavy-looking pewter pitcher on the table and whack him with that. Or kick him, or punch him, or whatever she had to do to get back out that kitchen door. She was as tall as he was, probably almost as strong, and certainly faster. She was half his age, a well-conditioned athlete. With the element of surprise on her side she had every chance of getting away. Once outside, she'd take off across the fields. He would never catch her.

Of course, all this did leave one little factor still working to his advantage: the gun. But the gun, so she now thought, could be discounted.

She had reached this conclusion during those last few minutes of leisurely, floating thought in the trunk of the car. She had been brooding about the strange contents of his toolbox and she had come to the realization that it was nothing but a box of props. There was just no other explanation for the handcuffs. The gun, the cuffs, whatever else he had in there—they were all part of the act, there to be used for show during the kidnapping. Apparently, however, Jackie and Darlene had decided during their final planning that it was safer to make the operation simpler and less theatrical.

And if the gun was merely a stage prop, then surely they wouldn't have been crazy enough to load it with live ammunition. That would have been unthinkably—and unnecessarily—dangerous. Guns can be fired accidentally, they can be dropped and go off. No, there were blanks in there. That was why he hadn't hit Peg. That was why the report of the gun had been so unimpressive. That was why . . .

The cuff came loose. Lee dropped her hands to her sides and moved forward. *Stop thinking now. Leave it to your instincts, your muscles, not your brain. Act.*

She took one slow, subdued step. A second one. Jackie began following her. Another step. Another. She put her right hand around her left wrist as if massaging it. She slowed her stride imperceptibly, enough to let him come within range. When he did, she pivoted, exactly as if she were on the tee driving for maximum distance: pulling with all the power and torque of the left side of her body—hip, torso, and shoulder—her left arm extended and propped by the hand around her wrist.

Given the circumstances, it was a heck of a swing, a 250-yarder, and it was lucky for her that it was, because Jackie, his reflexes as quick as a squirrel's, saw it coming and jerked down and toward her, turning his head to the side and managing to get inside the glittering arc of the cuffs. As a result Lee caught him not with the metal bracelets but with her forearm. But she caught him hard, on the bridge of the nose, with the bony part of her arm just above the wrist. Her arm felt as if someone had hit it with a hammer, and Jackie grunted and fell back, stumbling and finally falling over his own feet.

Lee didn't wait to see him hit the floor, didn't stop for the pewter pitcher, didn't do anything but streak for the doorway. She already had ten feet on him and he had yet to get to his feet. There was no way—

The Toby jug on the shelf two feet from her head—she had noticed it on the way in because her great-aunt had one like it, a little man in a cocked hat holding a mug of ale on his knee—broke into pieces, one of which flicked her cheek. Seemingly at the same moment there was an ear-splitting, wall-rattling CRACK. Petrified, she stopped instantly. Her eyes involuntarily snapped shut. When she opened them and looked at the spot where the Toby jug had stood, she saw what she expected to see: in the dun-colored wall behind the shelf was a small, black hole, perfectly round except for where the plaster had crumbled around the rim.

She had made a slight miscalculation. The gun was loaded.

"You win," she said weakly, turning slowly around with her hands raised. "I'll do what you say."

"Really, I wish you would," Jackie said, rubbing his nose. "This is getting annoying."

✳   ✳   ✳

Graham waved his thanks to the pilot, swung his bag over his shoulder, and slipped out of the twin-engine plane that had brought him from Boston after his morning flight from Toronto. Smiling, he scanned the passenger area of the Block Island terminal, looking for Lee.

"Nuts," he said aloud when he didn't find her. But he wasn't really all that surprised. She did have a job to do, after all; she couldn't just take off anytime she felt like it. He'd see her soon enough. He smiled again, thinking about what he was going to tell her when he had a chance to sit her down for a while. First things first, however: he'd have to call from the terminal for a rental car—

"Graham?"

It took him a moment to place the seamed, jowly face of the man who had placed his hand on his arm. Then he brightened. "Why, hi, Arnie, I wasn't expecting to be greeted by the chief of—" But the look in Tolliver's eyes sobered him instantly. "What is it, Arnie? What's wrong?"

"We got ourselves a little problem," the chief said.

Chapter 20

On the drive to the police station, Tolliver brought Graham up to date. As soon as Peg had contacted them, Tolliver and one of his men had gone out to the golf course. There was nothing there. The Personal Plane Partner still lay on its back, spraddle-legged and ridiculous. Lee's and Peg's cars were still in the parking area, but Jackie's car was gone. Obviously he had taken Lee away with him.

"Blood?" Graham asked in a voice that barely made it out of his throat.

"No. No blood, no cartridges, no sign of violence. We're pretty sure she's all right, Graham. We think he means to use her as a hostage if he has to, to get off the island."

"We, who's we?"

"Well, me."

"Jesus, Arnie," Graham said, hardly able to make himself take it in. He was as frightened, as out-and-out, sick-to-the-stomach terror-stricken, as he'd ever been in his life. "When did this happen?"

"Less than an hour ago. Peg Fiske got hold of me from somebody's house out on the bluffs. I drove here straight from the golf course myself. One of my people is still out there."

"What have you done so far? Who have you contacted? Are you getting some help from the state? What about the FBI?"

Chief Tolliver glanced at him as he turned the black departmental car into the police station lot. "Whoa, take it easy. I made sure he hasn't left the island by boat or plane. Other than that, I haven't done a hell of a lot of anything. I just told you, I came straight from the golf course."

"You mean you haven't even—"

"I figured you're the man to talk to. Seems to me I remember hearing you're the big expert in this kind of thing." He switched off the engine. "From you, as I recall."

Graham glared at him. Easy enough for Tolliver to make his cornball little jokes. It was just another day to him, just another case folder. "Dammit, Arnie!"

"Take it easy, son," Tolliver said. "It's not gonna do anybody any good to get excited. I want your help on this. If you can't ease up a little, you're no damn good to me. Now, you want to get in on this or don't you?"

"Are you serious? Naturally I want—"

"Then take a deep breath and look at this like the professional you're supposed to be. Tell me what in the hell I do next."

Graham nodded, then breathed in deeply, and slowly let the air out. "Okay, Chief, I'm sorry. You're right, of course. It's just a little different when you're personally involved."

"Well, of course it is."

"Okay, first thing: have you heard from Piper? Any telephone calls, any—"

Tolliver shook his head. "Nothing."

"Well, it's early yet." He chewed on his lip. "Look, we've got to try to find out where they are. Now, this island isn't all that big—"

"Oh, I know where they are."

Graham stared. "You *know* where they are?"

"Well, I think so."

"But how?"

"You really want to waste time hearing how I know, or you want to step inside and go get us a plan?"

Graham, feeling his confidence and optimism beginning to return, managed something close to a smile. "Chief, you're really something else. Let's go get us a plan."

*   *   *

The seven men sat at one of the big conference tables in the community room. Graham was at one end and Tolliver, billowing acrid smoke from his pipe (when among his law enforcement colleagues rather than private citizens, he was merciless in his choice of tobacco), at the other. In the remaining five seats were the uniformed sergeant and corporal, the town attorney, and two young reserve officers, also in uniform at Graham's request. He had learned in the past that the more visible uniforms there were in a situation like this, the more peaceably things were likely to work out.

He had just outlined for them the plan that he and Tolliver had gotten their heads together on a few minutes before, in which Graham would show up at the cottage pretending to be a maintenance man of some kind and try to get Jackie to come outside by himself, where the uniformed officers would be ranged about, out of sight, waiting to make the arrest. Tolliver had contacted the owner of the cottage, a Newport architect who had bought it a couple of years ago and was currently operating it as a rental, with eventual renovation in mind. He had been happy to fax pictures of the house and grounds to the island, so that they now had an accurate idea of the layout. Fortunately for them the two windows on the windward side were boarded up, so the police could come up and station themselves without being seen. Once they were in place, Graham would drive right up to the house in a beat-up pickup truck and knock on the door. From there on it was up to him.

"Anyone got any questions?" the chief asked.

Heads shook. Murmurs of approval were heard. "Sounds good." "Let's go do it." "Let's go get us a bad guy."

Only the town attorney, a portly, baby-faced man with jet-black eyebrows, a pendulous lower lip, and a decidedly lawyerly manner, demurred. "I have no objection to the plan as such, but under no circumstances should Mr. Sheldon participate directly. Should anything happen, the legal and insurance complications would be prodigious. What's more, the warrant that's been sworn out would be compromised. I'm afraid someone else will have to take his part."

"Who would you suggest?" the chief asked.

"Well, anyone else at the table. On second thought, it had better be none of the reserve officers either, just to be on the safe side."

"That leaves me, Sergeant Cuneo, and Corporal Goff," Tolliver pointed out, "and Piper knows all of us; we couldn't get away with it. But he's never talked to Graham, he doesn't know his voice. No, it's got to be Graham."

"That's all well and good, Chief, but the liability provisions are explicit on this point, and—"

"Screw the liability provisions," Tolliver said. "We got a life at stake here."

"Very well, but I want to be on record—"

"*Could we get on with it, please?*" Graham demanded, more forcefully than he had intended. He was doing his best to stay cool, as if this were merely some consulting assignment, but it wasn't some abstract, faceless life at stake, it was *Lee's* life, didn't these people realize that? He had sat through the briefing on pins and needles, painfully eager to get going, to do *something.* Who knew what Piper might do if he got desperate, who knew what he had already done to her, what he might be doing or planning to do this very minute? Who knew—

Who knew anything, when it came down to it? an insinuating voice whispered from some webbed and shadowy corner of his mind. *Who could say, for a fact, that she was actually in the cottage, or even that she was still alive? Who could say for sure that she wasn't already—*

He startled the others by slamming his hand on the table and standing up. "If there's nothing else, I think we should get under way."

"We better stop by the equipment room and put on some body armor," one of the reserve officers said. "You never know, the guy might get stupid."

"*No!*" Graham practically shouted, then pulled himself together. "No," he said again, this time more reasonably, "I don't want any armor, I don't want that kind of mentality, I don't even want that thought in our minds. No blazing guns, no flying bullets. This isn't a raid, this isn't a siege. It's a fake-out, a con job; we're going to do it peacefully. If it doesn't work, I just turn around and leave quietly, and we come back later, and that will be the time for bullhorns and body armor. Now let's get going."

He realized from the uncomfortable glances around the table that he was blatantly usurping Tolliver's authority. "That is," he added contritely, "if the chief agrees,"

Tolliver laughed. "You mean I get a say in this too? Well, all right." He pushed himself heavily to his feet. "Then I say it's time to get this show the hell on the road."

Chapter 21

"Will you stop fidgeting?" Jackie said, his voice rising to a squeak. "You're driving me nuts. You want something to eat? You want some coffee?"

"No. I'm fidgeting because I can't get comfortable," Lee said.

It was five o'clock, she had been sitting on the cracked, bumpy linoleum floor, handcuffed to the radiator, for two hours, and she was getting grumpy. She was able to support her shoulders against the wall, but not comfortably. Her back ached, and the base of her spine was sore.

"And I have to go to the bathroom."

"Not by yourself," he said, a condition he had laid down before, which she had refused and now refused again. She didn't have to use the bathroom anyway; she was just tired of being cooped up and helpless. She wanted another chance to make a run for it, to blindside Jackie, to do *anything*.

"At least unhook me from this thing so I can stand up for a minute."

"Not on your life. Do I look stupid or something? I may be crazy, but I'm not nuts."

"Jackie, what are you going to do?"

"I *told* you, I don't know. I have to work things out."

"What good will it do—"

"Will you shut up already? Criminy, don't you ever stop talking? Can't you just cry or something for a while?"

Restlessly he jumped up from the table and took the wall-hung telephone into the kitchen for the umpteenth time since they had gotten there, pulling on the already stretched-out cord. He spoke with his hand over his mouth so she couldn't hear clearly, but she heard enough to know that he'd been trying to contact Darlene all afternoon. At first he had called the various hotels to find out where she was staying and soon learned she was at the National. Since then he had unsuccessfully called every few minutes, refusing to leave a number.

Unsuccessful again, he came into the living room, anxious and jumpy, stopping cold at the sound of an approaching vehicle on the road. They both listened alertly, as they had every other time anything had come near. The other cars and trucks had all passed and faded into the distance, but not this one. They heard it slow down, then turn onto the gravel driveway. Jackie went cautiously to one of the windows, looking out through the space beside the pulled-down window shade.

"A pickup truck," he said under his breath. He stepped back from the window and leveled his finger at her. "If you make a noise . . . if you do *anything* . . . I don't have anything to lose, Lee, I'm warning you."

The truck door creaked loudly open, clunked, groaned again, and slammed shut. For a while there were no other sounds.

"He's looking at some damn clipboard," Jackie said to himself. "Come on, come on, come on, just get going, dammit, you're at the wrong house."

She heard the slow crunch of footsteps, another long pause, and then a casual *tap-tap* at the door. She held her breath. Jackie looked as if he'd explode if you stuck a pin in him.

Another knock. She could hear a tuneless, breathy whistle from the other side of the door. A third knock, more forceful, and then an irritated mutter: "Aw, hell."

She stiffened, her ears pricking like a dog's.

Graham?

The doorknob rattled. "Hey! Anybody home?"

Yes, Graham, for sure! My God! Every nerve in her body seemed to leap. She glanced at Jackie, then quickly looked down at the floor for fear of giving everything away.

She heard the jangle of a ring of keys from outside, the agonizingly slow process of going through them—if it went on much longer she was going to burst out of her skin—and finally the choosing of the right one and the shake of the ring to free it.

The key scraped in the lock. The doorknob jiggled again.

*   *   *

Graham wiggled the key in the lock and shook the knob some more. He knew the door wasn't going to open because he didn't have the right key, but if Piper was inside, the commotion ought to be getting a rise out of him.

"Hell," he grumbled again, pulling out the key and shaking the ring some more, as if he planned to go through all fifty or so until he found the one he was looking for.

The knob turned on its own. Graham took a step back, slouched a little more, twirled the toothpick he'd stuck between his teeth. "How ya doin'," he said as the door opened a few inches.

"What can I do for you?" Piper asked.

"Hey, I thought you weren't home," Graham said. "I'm Mike from Bug-Out Pest Control?"

Jackie's one visible eye squinted at him. "We don't have any bugs here."

"Mr. Farley has me do this two times a year, spring and fall. Carpenter ants, you know? I gotta get in the shed."

"The shed?"

Graham pointed to an outbuilding fifty yards from the house.

"So go ahead," Jackie said, "what's the problem?"

Graham sighed and shifted the toothpick to the opposite corner of his mouth, "Look, mac, I'm sorry to bother you, but I need the key."

"I don't know anything about any key. I'm just renting. You'll have to come back later." He started to close the door.

"It's in the right-hand cupboard over the sink. I know where it is, I can get it." He pushed on the door.

Jackie held fast. "Look, this isn't a great time for me. I don't feel too well. I was sleeping."

"Hey, I'm sorry, buddy, you want me to get a doctor?"

"I don't need a doctor, I just need to get some rest, okay? Just come back later. Tomorrow."

With his right hand Graham kept the door from closing. "Then you got to sign this sheet saying I was here." Graham knew that he was pushing; he could sense Jackie's growing mistrust. "Look, mister, it's just that I got this contract—"

"I'm sorry. This just isn't the time. Find someplace else to spray, okay?"

"Okay, okay." God, he hated to give it up, to have to fall back on a full-fledged raid with inherent risks of miscommunication, accidents, and foul-ups. "I'm going, I'm going," he said, backing off, but putting just the tiniest edge of puzzlement and suspicion into his voice in hopes of getting Jackie to keep the conversation going, to give him a little more time.

"All right . . . wait up," Jackie said. He opened the door a little wider. "Come on in."

*   *   *

The flood of relief that had swept through her at the first sound of Graham's voice had ebbed away, to be replaced by a freezing sense of dread as the two men's wary conversation continued. Her first thought had been to let Graham know that she was there: to rattle the handcuffs against the radiator, to break the window above her head with her shoe, even to call out, but she had quickly decided against it. Jackie was as tightly wound as a rubber strap on one of his nutty training devices, and she was afraid that anything sudden might make him shoot them both in a blind panic. Graham wouldn't have a chance. Jackie was standing at the entry with only his head visible from the outside, so Graham had no way of knowing that he was nervously clutching the gun, fingers twitching, in his raised right hand, hidden from Graham by the doorjamb, but no more than a foot from his head. And Graham, if he was armed at all, certainly wasn't standing there pretending to be Mike from Bug-Out Pest Control with a gun in his hand or anywhere in sight.

So she kept quiet. But she didn't keep still. The radiator to which her wrist was hooked was about seven feet down the wall from the door, and while they went on with their edgy sparring, she inched her body along the floor toward Jackie until she had stretched as far as her shackled left wrist would let her. With Jackie's face stuck in the opening of the door, she thought that if she could get within range, she could lash out with her foot and slam the door on his head. If she put everything she had into it, surely she could stun him enough to let Graham take the initiative, or maybe even knock him unconscious.

But she couldn't make it. With the door open less than a foot, it was impossible. Lying full-length on the floor with her arm about to pop from its socket she could just reach it with her toe, but it was at an angle and there was no way for her to thrust against it with any power.

Until Jackie called Graham back. "All right . . . wait up." He opened the door a little wider. "Come on in."

Lee launched herself, pushing off partly against the radiator with her left hand and partly against the floor with her elbow and hip. She actually got herself airborne, like a Cossack dancer, and managed to let fly, all out, with both feet at the same time.

The door snapped sharply forward, whacking Jackie's head just in front of the ears.

"*Aik!*"

All in the space of a second, the door whanged back open against the soles of her feet, Graham's hands—she hadn't realized she knew by heart the look of his strong hands, his muscular wrists—seized on Jackie's collar and yanked, and Jackie went flying—literally flying, his feet ten inches off the floor— out the door and out of sight. Behind him the gun dropped to the floor as if it was all that was left of him after a magic-show disappearance.

There was a flurry of confused scuffling outside, and several male voices, Chief Tolliver's among them, all shouting at once, and then Graham was there kneeling beside her, his eyes so ablaze with naked worry it made her heart twist with guilt and with pleasure.

"Lee! Are you—"

"I'm all right, I'm fine," she said quickly. "He didn't hurt me."

He sighed and sat back on his heels, shaking his head. He took a long look at her lying there on the floor of the old cottage, sweaty and disheveled, shackled by a pair of handcuffs to a peeling radiator.

"I'm certainly glad," he said, "that you've been keeping out of trouble."

"Well, really, it's not as if it's my fault," she said.

They looked at each other, then bent their heads together so that their foreheads touched, and laughed, from deep inside, until their sides ached.

Chapter 22

Leaning back against the bench, Lee stretched her legs out in front of her, wriggling her toes inside the old sneakers and practically purring with contentment. Her eyes were closed, her face turned up to the welcome warmth of the morning sun. She twisted her neck to one side and then the other just for the pleasure of feeling her muscles contract.

Behind and below her, she could hear the lazy slap-and-gurgle of water against wooden pilings. Her nostrils were filled with the tang of the sea and the sharp, oddly pleasant bite of creosote. The sun soaked its way through her shirt and into her shoulders, easing away the last of the morning chill.

"Aaahhh," she said.

"Would you like me to tell you exactly what you're thinking?" Peg asked from a few feet away.

They were on the dock waiting for the early ferry to begin loading. Peg would be taking it back to Galilee, then driving to the Providence airport to leave the car and catch her flight to Albuquerque. Lee and Graham would be remaining behind to treat themselves to their promised minivacation. While Graham had gone across the street to get coffee for the three of them, Lee and Peg had left the car in line and gone to the edge of the dock, Lee to sit stretching in the sun like a cat on a January day, and Peg to stand at the railing and light up a cigarillo. It was the first time Lee had ever seen her smoke, although Peg had told her that she had once been a two-pack-a-day cigarette smoker. Thoughtfully she was standing downwind of Lee.

"All right, I'll bite," Lee said, her eyes still closed. "What am I thinking?"

"You're thinking it's really great to be alive."

Lee opened her eyes, blinking in the sunlight. She hadn't realized it herself—she'd been under the impression she wasn't thinking of anything at all—but Peg was right. "Well, things did get a little scary for a while there yesterday."

Peg nodded and drew on her cigarillo, but it had gone out. She dropped it, half-smoked, into a litter can and came to sit beside Lee, looking troubled and somber, not at all her typical expression. "Lee . . ." she began, staring at her hands.

"Want me to tell you what you have on *your* mind?" Lee asked.

Peg lifted her head to look at her.

"You're feeling guilty about taking off and leaving me with Jackie yesterday," Lee said. "You're wondering if it was the right thing to do."

"Well, yes."

"It was," Lee told her firmly. "In the first place, Jackie was trying his best to kill you at the time, if you remember. Fortunately he couldn't shoot straight."

"I know," Peg said miserably, "but—"

"And in the second place, what would have happened if you'd given up and come back? He'd have had us both, that's what. The only hope I had was for you to get away and get help. You know what I was afraid of? That you'd decide to act what you thought was noble and that you *wouldn't* run."

Peg's eyes lifted to meet Lee's. "I hope you mean that."

"Of course I mean it," Lee said with honest warmth. "Now, stop being such a jerk, and come out and admit that what really bothers you is missing out on being in the middle of all the excitement later on."

This was the kind of pep talk Lee was used to getting from Peg, not giving to her. It was nice to return the favor for once.

One corner of Peg's mouth went up in a half-smile. "Well, there is that, yes," she said. "Dammit." They both laughed and settled back, with the air cleared, to bask in the sun a little more.

* * *

It *was* good to be alive. There had been a few moments the day before when Lee had been certain that she wouldn't be around to see this morning's sun. During the two wretched hours she had been chained to the radiator while an increasingly manic Jackie paced the floor, and talked to himself, and tried without success to reach Darlene, she had had a lot of time to wonder just what it was that he had in mind.

Now, of course, she knew. Nothing. He had no idea what he was going to do; he barely knew if he was coming or going. He had panicked at the golf range and he had run, with her in tow, to what he thought was the only safe place on the island, while he tried to figure out what was going on. Why had Darlene returned to the island? Why had she confessed? Was she free? In jail? Had she admitted only to the phony kidnapping or to the murder too? Had she or hadn't she implicated him? All these concerns and more he had blathered to Tolliver at the police station, notwithstanding the chief's meticulous reading to him of his rights (including the right to remain silent), and despite the presence of Graham, Lee, and Sergeant Cuneo in the chief's office. In the relief of having it all over with, Jackie simply couldn't stop talking.

It had never been his idea, he raved, while waiting for a local lawyer to arrive; it was Darlene who had talked him into it, and only into the "foolproof" plan for the kidnapping, at that. He had never—he wanted that clearly understood—*never* intended Stuart's death. It was only that things started to go so wildly wrong from the moment the kidnapping had gone awry—here he paused long enough for his own poisonous glance at Lee—and then had gone from bad to worse, getting more out of hand by the minute. When Stuart pieced together the kidnapping plot and who had been behind it, Darlene went to pieces and insisted to Jackie that her husband had to be done away with.

At this point Graham had been unable to resist a wry comment. "I see," he said. "It was all Darlene's idea, not yours. She forced you into it."

"Absolutely!" Jackie had affirmed, eyes glowing with moral zeal. "I was completely against it."

"And the killing itself?" Graham went on. "Who was responsible for that, you or Darlene?"

"Well, that depends on what you mean by—"

"And who drove the spike in his throat?"

"Ah, mm . . ." Jackie hesitated, probably pondering just how much modern forensic science had been able to extract from the crime scene. "Well," he allowed, "technically I guess you'd have to say it was me who actually *did* it. But she was driving me out of my mind. You have no idea what that woman's like!"

At that point the attorney showed up and managed, with some difficulty, to shut Jackie down and get him out of the office and into the one-cell jail. Afterward, alone with a tired Lee and Graham once they had given their statements, Tolliver answered their questions. Why, they wondered, did he think that Darlene had suddenly come in from Boston and confessed to the kidnapping ruse? Easy, said the chief. Felix Grumbo, the bungling mock-kidnapper, who—based on Lee's description—had been a suspect from almost the start of the investigation, had been located and questioned by the police in Providence a day earlier and had blurted out the whole story, or as much of it as he knew. Although he had never seen Jackie, but only spoken with him on the telephone, he was able and more than willing to finger Darlene. Somehow, Darlene had gotten wind of this and had hurriedly flown to Block Island to "voluntarily" confess to her part in the fake kidnapping before she was formally confronted with it and necessarily implicated in the murder.

It was the garrulous Felix who had also unwittingly provided the chief with Jackie and Lee's whereabouts. Where else, after all, would Jackie run, if not to the rented, isolated cottage that had been Felix's base of operations?

"I tell you the one thing I still can't get a read on, though," Tolliver said, digging with his pipe in his tobacco pouch. "Why would she come down here and talk to me like that without ever letting her boyfriend in on it? That just doesn't make any sense."

"I think I can explain that," Lee said.

"I don't doubt it for a minute," mused Graham.

"You see, Jackie was in Southampton yesterday and this morning. Darlene probably didn't know where to get hold of him, but she couldn't wait any more. If she was to beat Felix to the punch by confessing to the hoax, she had no choice but to talk to you as soon as possible."

Tolliver lit up, leaned back in his creaky swivel chair, and watched a thick, lazy cloud of smoke drift up to the ceiling while he considered.

"Makes sense to me," he said.

*　*　*

At about the time the sound of the cars in the ferry line start-ing their engines brought Lee and Peg out of their sun-and-sea-induced stupors, Graham appeared with three cardboard cups fitted into a carrier. "Sorry to take so long. There was quite a line; the *latte* craze seems to have made it to Block Island."

"Thanks, Graham," Peg said, taking hers. "I'll have it in the boat with my Danish. They're starting to load. Oh, before I for-get." She reached into her bag and came up with a folded sheet of paper that she handed to Lee.

"What's this?" Lee asked.

"That's my order for five hundred and seventy-five bucks' worth of Stroke-Cutters. I don't see why you shouldn't get the commission."

"Peg, you have to be kidding."

"No, why would I be kidding?"

"For one thing, I doubt very much whether Jackie's firm is in business anymore."

"Well, we don't know that, do we? What's the harm in send-ing it in for me?"

Lee laughed. "I can't believe you're serious. After what he did—"

"So what? Just because somebody tried to kill me doesn't mean he can't help my golf game. Oops, they're loading—back-ward again! Wish me luck."

A quick embrace with Lee, a slightly more formal one with Graham, and she was gone.

Graham and Lee sat on the bench and uncapped their coffees.

"Whew," Graham said, "do we truly have two whole days all to ourselves?"

"Sure do," said Lee with a smile, but the truth of it was that it didn't sound like very much. Early Monday morning—the day after tomorrow—she'd be off to compete in the qualifying round at Brookline. When would they see each other next?

"Ah, coffee's good," Graham said. "Still hot. Oh, by the way, I think it's a good idea. Let's do it."

"Do what?" Lee said absently. She was watching Peg stop-and-start-and-jerk her way onto the ferry.

"Get ourselves engaged," Graham said casually.

For a moment she couldn't speak but only stare at him. "You—you *heard* me!"

He was laughing. "Naturally I heard you. I can hear two people at once."

"But you didn't—you never—why didn't you—"

"I had to think about it. There were decisions to be made. For example, I had to give some thought as to whether or not an engagement ring would be appropriate."

"But—but—I mean, but—"

"Calm down, will you?" He moved her hand with its cup toward her mouth. "Drink some coffee, will you? *Slowly,* now."

She did, making herself take two long swallows while she tried to collect her thoughts. "Why wouldn't an engagement ring be appropriate?"

"Well, I saw a magazine article a little while ago where it was described as an anachronistic symbol of possession from the bad old days when a man was considered to be a woman's lord and master. I guess some people think it's a pretty old-fashioned kind of thing—and you're not exactly an old-fashioned girl, you know."

"But I *am* old-fashioned—sort of. I just happen to have a thing about golf, that's all." She drank some more coffee, only now beginning to fully realize what was happening. Good gosh, she was engaged! To Graham!

"Is that true?" he asked. "You're old-fashioned? Romantic?" He tilted his head, giving her the full, shivery treatment with those lucid blue eyes. "Sentimental, even?"

"*Yes!*"

"Well, that's good," he said, and calmly, quizzically watched her as she mechanically downed her coffee, sip by sip.

"Graham," she said, puzzled by his manner, "what are you—" She stopped as something metallic touched her lip. She lowered the cup. "You didn't." For the first time she laughed. "Did you, really?"

He shrugged happily. "I guess it's a little corny, isn't it? And if I remember right, it's supposed to be a crystal glass of champagne, not a cardboard cup of *caffè latte.* But I thought you wouldn't mind."

By now she had fished it out of the coffee, a pretty, tastefully modest diamond set among a ring of smaller stones on a silver band. "It's wonderful," she said thickly. "It's—"

"I'll take that as an acceptance," Graham said. "Now, then. This engagement stuff is new to me. Am I supposed to give you a present?"

"I don't know, it's new to me too."

"Well, I think I'd like to. Why don't you think about what you'd like for an engagement present?"

"I already know what I'd like for an engagement present," she said tentatively.

He gave her his easy smile and took her hand. "Go ahead and name it, babe."

"All right. A graphite-shafted King Cobra sixty-degree lob wedge with a sixty-three-degree lie and a thirteen-degree bounce." She was laughing again. "Unless, of course, *you* think that's too sentimental."